Madame Bovary

Madame Bovary

Gustave Flaubert

MINT EDITIONS

Madame Bovary was first published in 1856.

This edition published by Mint Editions 2020.

ISBN 9781513264981 | E-ISBN 9781513265667

Published by Mint Editions®

 MINT
EDITIONS

minteditionbooks.com

Publishing Director: Jennifer Newens
Project Manager: Gabrielle Maudiere
Design & Production: Rachel Lopez Metzger

PART 1

Chapter 1

We were in class when the head-master came in, followed by a "new fellow," not wearing the school uniform, and a school servant carrying a large desk. Those who had been asleep woke up, and every one rose as if just surprised at his work.

The head-master made a sign to us to sit down. Then, turning to the class-master, he said to him in a low voice—

"Monsieur Roger, here is a pupil whom I recommend to your care; he'll be in the second. If his work and conduct are satisfactory, he will go into one of the upper classes, as becomes his age."

The "new fellow," standing in the corner behind the door so that he could hardly be seen, was a country lad of about fifteen, and taller than any of us. His hair was cut square on his forehead like a village chorister's; he looked reliable, but very ill at ease. Although he was not broad-shouldered, his short school jacket of green cloth with black buttons must have been tight about the arm-holes, and showed at the opening of the cuffs red wrists accustomed to being bare. His legs, in blue stockings, looked out from beneath yellow trousers, drawn tight by braces, He wore stout, ill-cleaned, hob-nailed boots.

We began repeating the lesson. He listened with all his ears, as attentive as if at a sermon, not daring even to cross his legs or lean on his elbow; and when at two o'clock the bell rang, the master was obliged to tell him to fall into line with the rest of us.

When we came back to work, we were in the habit of throwing our caps on the ground so as to have our hands more free; we used from the door to toss them under the form, so that they hit against the wall and made a lot of dust: it was "the thing."

But, whether he had not noticed the trick, or did not dare to attempt it, the "new fellow," was still holding his cap on his knees even after prayers were over. It was one of those head-gears of composite order, in which we can find traces of the bearskin, shako, billycock hat, sealskin cap, and cotton night-cap; one of those poor things, in fine, whose dumb ugliness has depths of expression, like an imbecile's face. Oval, stiffened with whalebone, it began with three round knobs; then came in succession lozenges of velvet and rabbit-skin separated by a red band; after that a sort of bag that ended in a cardboard polygon covered with complicated braiding, from which hung, at the end of a long thin cord, small twisted gold threads in the manner of a tassel. The cap was new; its peak shone.

"Rise," said the master.

He stood up; his cap fell. The whole class began to laugh. He stooped to pick it up. A neighbor knocked it down again with his elbow; he picked it up once more.

"Get rid of your helmet," said the master, who was a bit of a wag.

There was a burst of laughter from the boys, which so thoroughly put the poor lad out of countenance that he did not know whether to keep his cap in his hand, leave it on the ground, or put it on his head. He sat down again and placed it on his knee.

"Rise," repeated the master, "and tell me your name."

The new boy articulated in a stammering voice an unintelligible name.

"Again!"

The same sputtering of syllables was heard, drowned by the tittering of the class.

"Louder!" cried the master; "louder!"

The "new fellow" then took a supreme resolution, opened an inordinately large mouth, and shouted at the top of his voice as if calling someone in the word "Charbovari."

A hubbub broke out, rose in crescendo with bursts of shrill voices (they yelled, barked, stamped, repeated "Charbovari! Charbovari"), then died away into single notes, growing quieter only with great difficulty, and now and again suddenly recommencing along the line of a form whence rose here and there, like a damp cracker going off, a stifled laugh.

However, amid a rain of impositions, order was gradually re-established in the class; and the master having succeeded in catching the name of "Charles Bovary," having had it dictated to him, spelt out, and re-read, at once ordered the poor devil to go and sit down on the punishment form at the foot of the master's desk. He got up, but before going hesitated.

"What are you looking for?" asked the master.

"My c-a-p," timidly said the "new fellow," casting troubled looks round him.

"Five hundred lines for all the class!" shouted in a furious voice stopped, like the *Quos ego**, a fresh outburst. "Silence!" continued the

---

* A quotation from the Aeneid signifying a threat.

master indignantly, wiping his brow with his handkerchief, which he had just taken from his cap. "As to you, 'new boy,' you will conjugate 'ridiculus sum'* twenty times."

Then, in a gentler tone, "Come, you'll find your cap again; it hasn't been stolen."

Quiet was restored. Heads bent over desks, and the "new fellow" remained for two hours in an exemplary attitude, although from time to time some paper pellet flipped from the tip of a pen came bang in his face. But he wiped his face with one hand and continued motionless, his eyes lowered.

In the evening, at preparation, he pulled out his pens from his desk, arranged his small belongings, and carefully ruled his paper. We saw him working conscientiously, looking up every word in the dictionary, and taking the greatest pains. Thanks, no doubt, to the willingness he showed, he had not to go down to the class below. But though he knew his rules passably, he had little finish in composition. It was the cure of his village who had taught him his first Latin; his parents, from motives of economy, having sent him to school as late as possible.

His father, Monsieur Charles Denis Bartolome Bovary, retired assistant-surgeon-major, compromised about 1812 in certain conscription scandals, and forced at this time to leave the service, had taken advantage of his fine figure to get hold of a dowry of sixty thousand francs that offered in the person of a hosier's daughter who had fallen in love with his good looks. A fine man, a great talker, making his spurs ring as he walked, wearing whiskers that ran into his moustache, his fingers always garnished with rings and dressed in loud colours, he had the dash of a military man with the easy go of a commercial traveller.

Once married, he lived for three or four years on his wife's fortune, dining well, rising late, smoking long porcelain pipes, not coming in at night till after the theatre, and haunting cafes. The father-in-law died, leaving little; he was indignant at this, "went in for the business," lost some money in it, then retired to the country, where he thought he would make money.

But, as he knew no more about farming than calico, as he rode his horses instead of sending them to plough, drank his cider in bottle instead of selling it in cask, ate the finest poultry in his farmyard, and

---

* I am ridiculous.

greased his hunting-boots with the fat of his pigs, he was not long in finding out that he would do better to give up all speculation.

For two hundred francs a year he managed to live on the border of the provinces of Caux and Picardy, in a kind of place half farm, half private house; and here, soured, eaten up with regrets, cursing his luck, jealous of everyone, he shut himself up at the age of forty-five, sick of men, he said, and determined to live at peace.

His wife had adored him once on a time; she had bored him with a thousand servilities that had only estranged him the more. Lively once, expansive and affectionate, in growing older she had become (after the fashion of wine that, exposed to air, turns to vinegar) ill-tempered, grumbling, irritable. She had suffered so much without complaint at first, until she had seem him going after all the village drabs, and until a score of bad houses sent him back to her at night, weary, stinking drunk. Then her pride revolted. After that she was silent, burying her anger in a dumb stoicism that she maintained till her death. She was constantly going about looking after business matters. She called on the lawyers, the president, remembered when bills fell due, got them renewed, and at home ironed, sewed, washed, looked after the workmen, paid the accounts, while he, troubling himself about nothing, eternally besotted in sleepy sulkiness, whence he only roused himself to say disagreeable things to her, sat smoking by the fire and spitting into the cinders.

When she had a child, it had to be sent out to nurse. When he came home, the lad was spoilt as if he were a prince. His mother stuffed him with jam; his father let him run about barefoot, and, playing the philosopher, even said he might as well go about quite naked like the young of animals. As opposed to the maternal ideas, he had a certain virile idea of childhood on which he sought to mould his son, wishing him to be brought up hardily, like a Spartan, to give him a strong constitution. He sent him to bed without any fire, taught him to drink off large draughts of rum and to jeer at religious processions. But, peaceable by nature, the lad answered only poorly to his notions. His mother always kept him near her; she cut out cardboard for him, told him tales, entertained him with endless monologues full of melancholy gaiety and charming nonsense. In her life's isolation she centered on the child's head all her shattered, broken little vanities. She dreamed of high station; she already saw him, tall, handsome, clever, settled as an engineer or in the law. She taught him to read, and even, on an old piano, she had taught him two or three little songs. But to all this

GUSTAVE FLAUBERT

Monsieur Bovary, caring little for letters, said, "It was not worth while. Would they ever have the means to send him to a public school, to buy him a practice, or start him in business? Besides, with cheek a man always gets on in the world." Madame Bovary bit her lips, and the child knocked about the village.

He went after the labourers, drove away with clods of earth the ravens that were flying about. He ate blackberries along the hedges, minded the geese with a long switch, went haymaking during harvest, ran about in the woods, played hop-scotch under the church porch on rainy days, and at great fetes begged the beadle to let him toll the bells, that he might hang all his weight on the long rope and feel himself borne upward by it in its swing. Meanwhile he grew like an oak; he was strong on hand, fresh of colour.

When he was twelve years old his mother had her own way; he began lessons. The cure took him in hand; but the lessons were so short and irregular that they could not be of much use. They were given at spare moments in the sacristy, standing up, hurriedly, between a baptism and a burial; or else the cure, if he had not to go out, sent for his pupil after the Angelus*. They went up to his room and settled down; the flies and moths fluttered round the candle. It was close, the child fell asleep, and the good man, beginning to doze with his hands on his stomach, was soon snoring with his mouth wide open. On other occasions, when Monsieur le Cure, on his way back after administering the viaticum to some sick person in the neighbourhood, caught sight of Charles playing about the fields, he called him, lectured him for a quarter of an hour and took advantage of the occasion to make him conjugate his verb at the foot of a tree. The rain interrupted them or an acquaintance passed. All the same he was always pleased with him, and even said the "young man" had a very good memory.

Charles could not go on like this. Madame Bovary took strong steps. Ashamed, or rather tired out, Monsieur Bovary gave in without a struggle, and they waited one year longer, so that the lad should take his first communion.

Six months more passed, and the year after Charles was finally sent to school at Rouen, where his father took him towards the end of October, at the time of the St. Romain fair.

---

* A devotion said at morning, noon, and evening, at the sound of a bell. Here, the evening prayer.

It would now be impossible for any of us to remember anything about him. He was a youth of even temperament, who played in playtime, worked in school-hours, was attentive in class, slept well in the dormitory, and ate well in the refectory. He had in loco parentis* a wholesale ironmonger in the Rue Ganterie, who took him out once a month on Sundays after his shop was shut, sent him for a walk on the quay to look at the boats, and then brought him back to college at seven o'clock before supper. Every Thursday evening he wrote a long letter to his mother with red ink and three wafers; then he went over his history note-books, or read an old volume of "Anarchasis" that was knocking about the study. When he went for walks he talked to the servant, who, like himself, came from the country.

By dint of hard work he kept always about the middle of the class; once even he got a certificate in natural history. But at the end of his third year his parents withdrew him from the school to make him study medicine, convinced that he could even take his degree by himself.

His mother chose a room for him on the fourth floor of a dyer's she knew, overlooking the Eau-de-Robec. She made arrangements for his board, got him furniture, table and two chairs, sent home for an old cherry-tree bedstead, and bought besides a small cast-iron stove with the supply of wood that was to warm the poor child.

Then at the end of a week she departed, after a thousand injunctions to be good now that he was going to be left to himself.

The syllabus that he read on the notice-board stunned him; lectures on anatomy, lectures on pathology, lectures on physiology, lectures on pharmacy, lectures on botany and clinical medicine, and therapeutics, without counting hygiene and materia medica—all names of whose etymologies he was ignorant, and that were to him as so many doors to sanctuaries filled with magnificent darkness.

He understood nothing of it all; it was all very well to listen—he did not follow. Still he worked; he had bound note-books, he attended all the courses, never missed a single lecture. He did his little daily task like a mill-horse, who goes round and round with his eyes bandaged, not knowing what work he is doing.

To spare him expense his mother sent him every week by the carrier a piece of veal baked in the oven, with which he lunched when he came back from the hospital, while he sat kicking his feet against the wall.

---

* In place of a parent.

After this he had to run off to lectures, to the operation-room, to the hospital, and return to his home at the other end of the town. In the evening, after the poor dinner of his landlord, he went back to his room and set to work again in his wet clothes, which smoked as he sat in front of the hot stove.

On the fine summer evenings, at the time when the close streets are empty, when the servants are playing shuttle-cock at the doors, he opened his window and leaned out. The river, that makes of this quarter of Rouen a wretched little Venice, flowed beneath him, between the bridges and the railings, yellow, violet, or blue. Working men, kneeling on the banks, washed their bare arms in the water. On poles projecting from the attics, skeins of cotton were drying in the air. Opposite, beyond the roots spread the pure heaven with the red sun setting. How pleasant it must be at home! How fresh under the beech-tree! And he expanded his nostrils to breathe in the sweet odours of the country which did not reach him.

He grew thin, his figure became taller, his face took a saddened look that made it nearly interesting. Naturally, through indifference, he abandoned all the resolutions he had made. Once he missed a lecture; the next day all the lectures; and, enjoying his idleness, little by little, he gave up work altogether. He got into the habit of going to the public-house, and had a passion for dominoes. To shut himself up every evening in the dirty public room, to push about on marble tables the small sheep bones with black dots, seemed to him a fine proof of his freedom, which raised him in his own esteem. It was beginning to see life, the sweetness of stolen pleasures; and when he entered, he put his hand on the door-handle with a joy almost sensual. Then many things hidden within him came out; he learnt couplets by heart and sang them to his boon companions, became enthusiastic about Beranger, learnt how to make punch, and, finally, how to make love.

Thanks to these preparatory labours, he failed completely in his examination for an ordinary degree. He was expected home the same night to celebrate his success. He started on foot, stopped at the beginning of the village, sent for his mother, and told her all. She excused him, threw the blame of his failure on the injustice of the examiners, encouraged him a little, and took upon herself to set matters straight. It was only five years later that Monsieur Bovary knew the truth; it was old then, and he accepted it. Moreover, he could not believe that a man born of him could be a fool.

So Charles set to work again and crammed for his examination, ceaselessly learning all the old questions by heart. He passed pretty well. What a happy day for his mother! They gave a grand dinner.

Where should he go to practice? To Tostes, where there was only one old doctor. For a long time Madame Bovary had been on the look-out for his death, and the old fellow had barely been packed off when Charles was installed, opposite his place, as his successor.

But it was not everything to have brought up a son, to have had him taught medicine, and discovered Tostes, where he could practice it; he must have a wife. She found him one—the widow of a bailiff at Dieppe—who was forty-five and had an income of twelve hundred francs. Though she was ugly, as dry as a bone, her face with as many pimples as the spring has buds, Madame Dubuc had no lack of suitors. To attain her ends Madame Bovary had to oust them all, and she even succeeded in very cleverly baffling the intrigues of a port-butcher backed up by the priests.

Charles had seen in marriage the advent of an easier life, thinking he would be more free to do as he liked with himself and his money. But his wife was master; he had to say this and not say that in company, to fast every Friday, dress as she liked, harass at her bidding those patients who did not pay. She opened his letter, watched his comings and goings, and listened at the partition-wall when women came to consult him in his surgery.

She must have her chocolate every morning, attentions without end. She constantly complained of her nerves, her chest, her liver. The noise of footsteps made her ill; when people left her, solitude became odious to her; if they came back, it was doubtless to see her die. When Charles returned in the evening, she stretched forth two long thin arms from beneath the sheets, put them round his neck, and having made him sit down on the edge of the bed, began to talk to him of her troubles: he was neglecting her, he loved another. She had been warned she would be unhappy; and she ended by asking him for a dose of medicine and a little more love.

Chapter 2

O ne night towards eleven o'clock they were awakened by the noise of a horse pulling up outside their door. The servant opened the garret-window and parleyed for some time with a man in the street below. He came for the doctor, had a letter for him. Natasie came downstairs shivering and undid the bars and bolts one after the other. The man left his horse, and, following the servant, suddenly came in behind her. He pulled out from his wool cap with grey top-knots a letter wrapped up in a rag and presented it gingerly to Charles, who rested on his elbow on the pillow to read it. Natasie, standing near the bed, held the light. Madame in modesty had turned to the wall and showed only her back.

This letter, sealed with a small seal in blue wax, begged Monsieur Bovary to come immediately to the farm of the Bertaux to set a broken leg. Now from Tostes to the Bertaux was a good eighteen miles across country by way of Longueville and Saint-Victor. It was a dark night; Madame Bovary junior was afraid of accidents for her husband. So it was decided the stable-boy should go on first; Charles would start three hours later when the moon rose. A boy was to be sent to meet him, and show him the way to the farm, and open the gates for him.

Towards four o'clock in the morning, Charles, well wrapped up in his cloak, set out for the Bertaux. Still sleepy from the warmth of his bed, he let himself be lulled by the quiet trot of his horse. When it stopped of its own accord in front of those holes surrounded with thorns that are dug on the margin of furrows, Charles awoke with a start, suddenly remembered the broken leg, and tried to call to mind all the fractures he knew. The rain had stopped, day was breaking, and on the branches of the leafless trees birds roosted motionless, their little feathers bristling in the cold morning wind. The flat country stretched as far as eye could see, and the tufts of trees round the farms at long intervals seemed like dark violet stains on the cast grey surface, that on the horizon faded into the gloom of the sky.

Charles from time to time opened his eyes, his mind grew weary, and, sleep coming upon him, he soon fell into a doze wherein, his recent sensations blending with memories, he became conscious of a double self, at once student and married man, lying in his bed as but now, and crossing the operation theatre as of old. The warm smell of poultices mingled in his brain with the fresh odour of dew; he heard the iron rings rattling along the curtain-rods of the bed and saw his wife sleeping. As he passed Vassonville he came upon a boy sitting on the grass at the edge of a ditch.

"Are you the doctor?" asked the child.

And on Charles's answer he took his wooden shoes in his hands and ran on in front of him.

The general practitioner, riding along, gathered from his guide's talk that Monsieur Rouault must be one of the well-to-do farmers.

He had broken his leg the evening before on his way home from a Twelfth-night feast at a neighbour's. His wife had been dead for two years. There was with him only his daughter, who helped him to keep house.

The ruts were becoming deeper; they were approaching the Bertaux.

The little lad, slipping through a hole in the hedge, disappeared; then he came back to the end of a courtyard to open the gate. The horse slipped on the wet grass; Charles had to stoop to pass under the branches. The watchdogs in their kennels barked, dragging at their chains. As he entered the Bertaux, the horse took fright and stumbled.

It was a substantial-looking farm. In the stables, over the top of the open doors, one could see great cart-horses quietly feeding from new racks. Right along the outbuildings extended a large dunghill, from which manure liquid oozed, while amidst fowls and turkeys, five or six peacocks, a luxury in Chauchois farmyards, were foraging on the top of it. The sheepfold was long, the barn high, with walls smooth as your hand. Under the cart-shed were two large carts and four ploughs, with their whips, shafts and harnesses complete, whose fleeces of blue wool were getting soiled by the fine dust that fell from the granaries. The courtyard sloped upwards, planted with trees set out symmetrically, and the chattering noise of a flock of geese was heard near the pond.

A young woman in a blue merino dress with three flounces came to the threshold of the door to receive Monsieur Bovary, whom she led to the kitchen, where a large fire was blazing. The servant's breakfast was boiling beside it in small pots of all sizes. Some damp clothes were drying inside the chimney-corner. The shovel, tongs, and the nozzle of the bellows, all of colossal size, shone like polished steel, while along the walls hung many pots and pans in which the clear flame of the hearth, mingling with the first rays of the sun coming in through the window, was mirrored fitfully.

Charles went up the first floor to see the patient. He found him in his bed, sweating under his bed-clothes, having thrown his cotton nightcap right away from him. He was a fat little man of fifty, with white skin and blue eyes, the forepart of his head bald, and he wore earrings. By his side on a chair stood a large decanter of brandy, whence he poured himself a little from time to time to keep up his spirits; but as soon as he caught sight of the doctor his elation subsided, and instead of swearing, as he had been doing for the last twelve hours, began to groan freely.

The fracture was a simple one, without any kind of complication.

Charles could not have hoped for an easier case. Then calling to mind the devices of his masters at the bedsides of patients, he comforted the sufferer with all sorts of kindly remarks, those caresses of the surgeon that are like the oil they put on bistouries. In order to make some splints a bundle of laths was brought up from the cart-house. Charles selected one, cut it into two pieces and planed it with a fragment of windowpane, while the servant tore up sheets to make bandages, and Mademoiselle Emma tried to sew some pads. As she was a long time before she found her work-case, her father grew impatient; she did not answer, but as she sewed she pricked her fingers, which she then put to her mouth to suck them. Charles was surprised at the whiteness of her nails. They were shiny, delicate at the tips, more polished than the ivory of Dieppe, and almond-shaped. Yet her hand was not beautiful, perhaps not white enough, and a little hard at the knuckles; besides, it was too long, with no soft inflections in the outlines. Her real beauty was in her eyes. Although brown, they seemed black because of the lashes, and her look came at you frankly, with a candid boldness.

The bandaging over, the doctor was invited by Monsieur Rouault himself to "pick a bit" before he left.

Charles went down into the room on the ground floor. Knives and forks and silver goblets were laid for two on a little table at the foot of a huge bed that had a canopy of printed cotton with figures representing Turks. There was an odour of iris-root and damp sheets that escaped from a large oak chest opposite the window. On the floor in corners were sacks of flour stuck upright in rows. These were the overflow from the neighbouring granary, to which three stone steps led. By way of decoration for the apartment, hanging to a nail in the middle of the wall, whose green paint scaled off from the effects of the saltpetre, was a crayon head of Minerva in gold frame, underneath which was written in Gothic letters "To dear Papa."

First they spoke of the patient, then of the weather, of the great cold, of the wolves that infested the fields at night.

Mademoiselle Rouault did not at all like the country, especially now that she had to look after the farm almost alone. As the room was chilly, she shivered as she ate. This showed something of her full lips, that she had a habit of biting when silent.

Her neck stood out from a white turned-down collar. Her hair, whose two black folds seemed each of a single piece, so smooth were they, was parted in the middle by a delicate line that curved slightly with the curve of the head; and, just showing the tip of the ear, it was joined behind in a thick chignon, with a wavy movement at the temples that the country doctor saw now for the first time in his life. The upper part of her cheek was rose-coloured. She had, like a man, thrust in between two buttons of her bodice a tortoise-shell eyeglass.

When Charles, after bidding farewell to old Rouault, returned to the room before leaving, he found her standing, her forehead against the window, looking into the garden, where the bean props had been knocked down by the wind. She turned round. "Are you looking for anything?" she asked.

"My whip, if you please," he answered.

He began rummaging on the bed, behind the doors, under the chairs. It had fallen to the floor, between the sacks and the wall. Mademoiselle Emma saw it, and bent over the flour sacks.

Charles out of politeness made a dash also, and as he stretched out his arm, at the same moment felt his breast brush against the back of the young girl bending beneath him. She drew herself up, scarlet, and looked at him over her shoulder as she handed him his whip.

Instead of returning to the Bertaux in three days as he had promised, he went back the very next day, then regularly twice a week, without counting the visits he paid now and then as if by accident.

Everything, moreover, went well; the patient progressed favourably; and when, at the end of forty-six days, old Rouault was seen trying to walk alone in his "den," Monsieur Bovary began to be looked upon as a man of great capacity. Old Rouault said that he could not have been cured better by the first doctor of Yvetot, or even of Rouen.

As to Charles, he did not stop to ask himself why it was a pleasure to him to go to the Bertaux. Had he done so, he would, no doubt, have attributed his zeal to the importance of the case, or perhaps to the money he hoped to make by it. Was it for this, however, that his visits to the farm formed a delightful exception to the meagre occupations of his life? On these days he rose early, set off at a gallop, urging on his horse, then got down to wipe his boots in the grass and put on black gloves before entering. He liked going into the courtyard, and noticing the gate turn against his shoulder, the cock crow on the wall, the lads run to meet him. He liked the granary and the stables; he liked old Rouault, who pressed his hand and called him his saviour; he liked the small wooden shoes of Mademoiselle Emma on the scoured flags of the kitchen—her high heels made her a little taller; and when she walked in front of him, the wooden soles springing up quickly struck with a sharp sound against the leather of her boots.

She always accompanied him to the first step of the stairs. When his horse had not yet been brought round she stayed there. They had said "Good-bye"; there was no more talking. The open air wrapped her round, playing with the soft down on the back of her neck, or blew to and fro on her hips the apron-strings, that fluttered like streamers. Once, during a thaw the bark of the trees in the yard was oozing, the snow on the roofs of the outbuildings was melting; she stood on the threshold, and went to fetch her sunshade and opened it. The sunshade of silk of the colour of pigeons' breasts, through which the sun shone, lighted up with shifting hues the white skin of her face. She smiled under the tender warmth, and drops of water could be heard falling one by one on the stretched silk.

During the first period of Charles's visits to the Bertaux, Madame Bovary junior never failed to inquire after the invalid, and she had even chosen in the book that she kept on a system of double entry a clean blank page for Monsieur Rouault. But when she heard he had a daughter, she began to make inquiries, and she learnt the Mademoiselle Rouault, brought up at the Ursuline Convent, had received what is called "a good education"; and so knew dancing, geography, drawing, how to embroider and play the piano. That was the last straw.

"So it is for this," she said to herself, "that his face beams when he goes to see her, and that he puts on his new waistcoat at the risk of spoiling it with the rain. Ah! that woman! That woman!"

And she detested her instinctively. At first she solaced herself by allusions that Charles did not understand, then by casual observations that he let pass for fear of a storm, finally by open apostrophes to which he knew not what to answer. "Why did he go back to the Bertaux now that Monsieur Rouault was cured and that these folks hadn't paid yet?

Ah! it was because a young lady was there, some one who know how to talk, to embroider, to be witty. That was what he cared about; he wanted town misses." And she went on—

"The daughter of old Rouault a town miss! Get out! Their grandfather was a shepherd, and they have a cousin who was almost had up at the assizes for a nasty blow in a quarrel. It is not worth while making such a fuss, or showing herself at church on Sundays in a silk gown like a countess. Besides, the poor old chap, if it hadn't been for the colza last year, would have had much ado to pay up his arrears."

For very weariness Charles left off going to the Bertaux. Heloise made him swear, his hand on the prayer-book, that he would go there no more after much sobbing and many kisses, in a great outburst of love. He obeyed then, but the strength of his desire protested against the servility of his conduct; and he thought, with a kind of naive hypocrisy, that his interdict to see her gave him a sort of right to love her. And then the widow was thin; she had long teeth; wore in all weathers a little black shawl, the edge of which hung down between her shoulder-blades; her bony figure was sheathed in her clothes as if they were a scabbard; they were too short, and displayed her ankles with the laces of her large boots crossed over grey stockings.

Charles's mother came to see them from time to time, but after a few days the daughter-in-law seemed to put her own edge on her, and then, like two knives, they scarified him with their reflections and observations. It was wrong of him to eat so much.

Why did he always offer a glass of something to everyone who came? What obstinacy not to wear flannels! In the spring it came about that a notary at Ingouville, the holder of the widow Dubuc's property, one fine day went off, taking with him all the money in his office. Heloise, it is true, still possessed, besides a share in a boat valued at six thousand francs, her house in the Rue St. Francois; and yet, with all this fortune that had been so trumpeted abroad, nothing, excepting perhaps a little furniture and a few clothes, had appeared in the household. The matter had to be gone into. The house at Dieppe was found to be eaten up with mortgages to its foundations; what she had placed with the notary God only knew, and her share in the boat did not exceed one thousand crowns. She had lied, the good lady! In his exasperation, Monsieur Bovary the elder, smashing a chair on the flags, accused his wife of having caused misfortune to the son by harnessing him to such a harridan, whose harness wasn't worth her hide. They came to Tostes. Explanations followed. There were scenes. Heloise in tears, throwing her arms about her husband, implored him to defend her from his parents.

Charles tried to speak up for her. They grew angry and left the house.

But "the blow had struck home." A week after, as she was hanging up some washing in her yard, she was seized with a spitting of blood, and the next day, while Charles had his back turned to her drawing the window-curtain, she said, "O God!" gave a sigh and fainted. She was dead! What a surprise! When all was over at the cemetery Charles went home. He found no one downstairs; he went up to the first floor to their room; saw her dress still hanging at the foot of the alcove; then, leaning against the writing-table, he stayed until the evening, buried in a sorrowful reverie. She had loved him after all!

Chapter 3

One morning old Rouault brought Charles the money for setting his leg—seventy-five francs in forty-sou pieces, and a turkey. He had heard of his loss, and consoled him as well as he could.

"I know what it is," said he, clapping him on the shoulder; "I've been through it. When I lost my dear departed, I went into the fields to be quite alone. I fell at the foot of a tree; I cried; I called on God; I talked nonsense to Him. I wanted to be like the moles that I saw on the branches, their insides swarming with worms, dead, and an end of it. And when I thought that there were others at that very moment with their nice little wives holding them in their embrace, I struck great blows on the earth with my stick. I was pretty well mad with not eating; the very idea of going to a cafe disgusted me—you wouldn't believe it. Well, quite softly, one day following another, a spring on a winter, and an autumn after a summer, this wore away, piece by piece, crumb by crumb; it passed away, it is gone, I should say it has sunk; for something always remains at the bottom as one would say—a weight here, at one's heart. But since it is the lot of all of us, one must not give way altogether, and, because others have died, want to die too. You must pull yourself together, Monsieur Bovary. It will pass away. Come to see us; my daughter thinks of you now and again, d'ye know, and she says you are forgetting her. Spring will soon be here. We'll have some rabbit-shooting in the warrens to amuse you a bit."

Charles followed his advice. He went back to the Bertaux. He found all as he had left it, that is to say, as it was five months ago. The pear trees were already in blossom, and Farmer Rouault, on his legs again, came and went, making the farm more full of life.

Thinking it his duty to heap the greatest attention upon the doctor because of his sad position, he begged him not to take his hat off, spoke to him in an undertone as if he had been ill, and even pretended to be angry because nothing rather lighter had been prepared for him than for the others, such as a little clotted cream or stewed pears. He told stories. Charles found himself laughing, but the remembrance of his wife suddenly coming back to him depressed him. Coffee was brought in; he thought no more about her.

He thought less of her as he grew accustomed to living alone. The new delight of independence soon made his loneliness bearable. He could now change his meal-times, go in or out without explanation, and when he was very tired stretch himself at full length on his bed. So he nursed and coddled himself and accepted the consolations that were offered him. On the other hand, the death of his wife had not served him ill in his business, since for a month people had been saying, "The poor young man! what a loss!" His name had been talked about, his practice had increased; and moreover, he could go to the Bertaux just as he liked. He had an aimless hope, and was vaguely happy; he thought himself better looking as he brushed his whiskers before the looking-glass.

One day he got there about three o'clock. Everybody was in the fields. He went into the kitchen, but did not at once catch sight of Emma; the outside shutters were closed. Through the chinks of the wood the sun sent across the flooring long fine rays that were broken at the corners of the furniture and trembled along the ceiling. Some flies on the table were crawling up the glasses that had been used, and buzzing as they drowned themselves in the dregs of the cider. The daylight that came in by the chimney made velvet of the soot at the back of the fireplace, and touched with blue the cold cinders. Between the window and the hearth Emma was sewing; she wore no fichu; he could see small drops of perspiration on her bare shoulders.

After the fashion of country folks she asked him to have something to drink. He said no; she insisted, and at last laughingly offered to have a glass of liqueur with him. So she went to fetch a bottle of curacao from the cupboard, reached down two small glasses, filled one to the brim, poured scarcely anything into the other, and, after having clinked glasses, carried hers to her mouth. As it was almost empty she bent back to drink, her head thrown back, her lips pouting, her neck on the strain. She laughed at getting none of it, while with the tip of her tongue passing between her small teeth she licked drop by drop the bottom of her glass.

She sat down again and took up her work, a white cotton stocking she was darning. She worked with her head bent down; she did not speak, nor did Charles. The air coming in under the door blew a little dust over the flags; he watched it drift along, and heard nothing but the throbbing in his head and the faint clucking of a hen that had laid an egg in the yard. Emma from time to time cooled her cheeks with the palms of her hands, and cooled these again on the knobs of the huge fire-dogs.

She complained of suffering since the beginning of the season from giddiness; she asked if sea-baths would do her any good; she began talking of her convent, Charles of his school; words came to them. They went up into her bedroom. She showed him her old music-books, the little prizes she had won, and the oak-leaf crowns, left at the bottom of a cupboard. She spoke to him, too, of her mother, of the country, and even showed him the bed in the garden where, on the first Friday of every month, she gathered flowers to put on her mother's tomb. But the gardener they had never knew anything about it; servants are so stupid! She would have dearly liked, if only for the winter, to live in town, although the length of the fine days made the country perhaps even more wearisome in the summer. And, according to what she was saying, her voice was clear, sharp, or, on a sudden all languor, drawn out in modulations that ended almost in murmurs as she spoke to herself, now joyous, opening big naive eyes, then with her eyelids half closed, her look full of boredom, her thoughts wandering.

Going home at night, Charles went over her words one by one, trying to recall them, to fill out their sense, that he might piece out the life she had lived before he knew her. But he never saw her in his thoughts other than he had seen her the first time, or as he had just left her. Then he asked himself what would become of her—if she would be married, and to whom! Alas! Old Rouault was rich, and she!—so beautiful! But Emma's face always rose before his eyes, and a monotone, like the humming of a top, sounded in his ears, "If you should marry after all! If you should marry!" At night he could not sleep; his throat was parched; he was athirst. He got up to drink from the water-bottle and opened the window. The night was covered with stars, a warm wind blowing in the distance; the dogs were barking. He turned his head towards the Bertaux.

Thinking that, after all, he should lose nothing, Charles promised himself to ask her in marriage as soon as occasion offered, but each time such occasion did offer the fear of not finding the right words sealed his lips.

Old Rouault would not have been sorry to be rid of his daughter, who was of no use to him in the house. In his heart he excused her, thinking her too clever for farming, a calling under the ban of Heaven, since one never saw a millionaire in it. Far from having made a fortune by it, the good man was losing every year; for if he was good in bargaining, in which he enjoyed the dodges of the trade, on the other hand, agriculture properly so called, and the internal management of the farm, suited him less than most people. He did not willingly take his hands out of his pockets, and did not spare expense in all that

GUSTAVE FLAUBERT

concerned himself, liking to eat well, to have good fires, and to sleep well. He liked old cider, underdone legs of mutton, glorias* well beaten up. He took his meals in the kitchen alone, opposite the fire, on a little table brought to him all ready laid as on the stage.

When, therefore, he perceived that Charles's cheeks grew red if near his daughter, which meant that he would propose for her one of these days, he chewed the cud of the matter beforehand. He certainly thought him a little meagre, and not quite the son-in-law he would have liked, but he was said to be well brought-up, economical, very learned, and no doubt would not make too many difficulties about the dowry. Now, as old Rouault would soon be forced to sell twenty-two acres of "his property," as he owed a good deal to the mason, to the harness-maker, and as the shaft of the cider-press wanted renewing, "If he asks for her," he said to himself, "I'll give her to him."

At Michaelmas Charles went to spend three days at the Bertaux.

The last had passed like the others in procrastinating from hour to hour. Old Rouault was seeing him off; they were walking along the road full of ruts; they were about to part. This was the time. Charles gave himself as far as to the corner of the hedge, and at last, when past it—

"Monsieur Rouault," he murmured, "I should like to say something to you."

They stopped. Charles was silent.

"Well, tell me your story. Don't I know all about it?" said old Rouault, laughing softly.

"Monsieur Rouault—Monsieur Rouault," stammered Charles.

"I ask nothing better", the farmer went on. "Although, no doubt, the little one is of my mind, still we must ask her opinion. So you get off—I'll go back home. If it is 'yes', you needn't return because of all the people about, and besides it would upset her too much. But so that you mayn't be eating your heart, I'll open wide the outer shutter of the window against the wall; you can see it from the back by leaning over the hedge."

And he went off.

Charles fastened his horse to a tree; he ran into the road and waited. Half an hour passed, then he counted nineteen minutes by his watch. Suddenly a noise was heard against the wall; the shutter had been thrown back; the hook was still swinging.

---

* A mixture of coffee and spirits.

The next day by nine o'clock he was at the farm. Emma blushed as he entered, and she gave a little forced laugh to keep herself in countenance. Old Rouault embraced his future son-in-law. The discussion of money matters was put off; moreover, there was plenty of time before them, as the marriage could not decently take place till Charles was out of mourning, that is to say, about the spring of the next year.

The winter passed waiting for this. Mademoiselle Rouault was busy with her trousseau. Part of it was ordered at Rouen, and she made herself chemises and nightcaps after fashion-plates that she borrowed. When Charles visited the farmer, the preparations for the wedding were talked over; they wondered in what room they should have dinner; they dreamed of the number of dishes that would be wanted, and what should be entrees.

Emma would, on the contrary, have preferred to have a midnight wedding with torches, but old Rouault could not understand such an idea. So there was a wedding at which forty-three persons were present, at which they remained sixteen hours at table, began again the next day, and to some extent on the days following.

Chapter 4

The guests arrived early in carriages, in one-horse chaises, two-wheeled cars, old open gigs, waggonettes with leather hoods, and the young people from the nearer villages in carts, in which they stood up in rows, holding on to the sides so as not to fall, going at a trot and well shaken up. Some came from a distance of thirty miles, from Goderville, from Normanville, and from Cany.

All the relatives of both families had been invited, quarrels between friends arranged, acquaintances long since lost sight of written to.

From time to time one heard the crack of a whip behind the hedge; then the gates opened, a chaise entered. Galloping up to the foot of the steps, it stopped short and emptied its load. They got down from all sides, rubbing knees and stretching arms. The ladies, wearing bonnets, had on dresses in the town fashion, gold watch chains, pelerines with the ends tucked into belts, or little coloured fichus fastened down behind with a pin, and that left the back of the neck bare. The lads, dressed like their papas, seemed uncomfortable in their new clothes (many that day hand-sewed their first pair of boots), and by their sides, speaking never a work, wearing the white dress of their first communion lengthened for the occasion were some big girls of fourteen or sixteen, cousins or elder sisters no doubt, rubicund, bewildered, their hair greasy with rose pomade, and very much afraid of dirtying their gloves. As there were not enough stable-boys to unharness all the carriages, the gentlemen turned up their sleeves and set about it themselves. According to their different social positions they wore tail-coats, overcoats, shooting jackets, cutaway-coats; fine tail-coats, redolent of family respectability, that only came out of the wardrobe on state occasions; overcoats with long tails flapping in the wind and round capes and pockets like sacks; shooting jackets of coarse cloth, generally worn with a cap with a brass-bound peak; very short cutaway-coats with two small buttons in the back, close together like a pair of eyes, and the tails of which seemed cut out of one piece by a carpenter's hatchet. Some, too (but these, you may be sure, would sit at the bottom of the table), wore their best blouses—that is to say, with collars turned down to the shoulders, the back gathered into small plaits and the waist fastened very low down with a worked belt.

And the shirts stood out from the chests like cuirasses! Everyone had just had his hair cut; ears stood out from the heads; they had been close-shaved; a few, even, who had had to get up before daybreak, and not been able to see to shave, had diagonal gashes under their noses or cuts the size of a three-franc piece along the jaws, which the fresh air en route had enflamed, so that the great white beaming faces were mottled here and there with red dabs.

The mairie was a mile and a half from the farm, and they went thither on foot, returning in the same way after the ceremony in the church. The procession, first united like one long coloured scarf that undulated across the fields, along the narrow path winding amid the green corn, soon lengthened out, and broke up into different groups that loitered to talk. The fiddler walked in front with his violin, gay with ribbons at its pegs. Then came the married pair, the relations, the friends, all following pell-mell; the children stayed behind amusing themselves plucking the bell-flowers from oat-ears, or playing amongst themselves unseen. Emma's dress, too long, trailed a little on the ground; from time to time she stopped to pull it up, and then delicately, with her gloved hands, she picked off the coarse grass and the thistledowns, while Charles, empty handed, waited till she had finished. Old Rouault, with a new silk hat and the cuffs of his black coat covering his hands up to the nails, gave his arm to Madame Bovary senior. As to Monsieur Bovary senior, who, heartily despising all these folk, had come simply in a frock-coat of military cut with one row of buttons—he was passing compliments of the bar to a fair young peasant. She bowed, blushed, and did not know what to say. The other wedding guests talked of their business or played tricks behind each other's backs, egging one another on in advance to be jolly. Those who listened could always catch the squeaking of the fiddler, who went on playing across the fields. When he saw that the rest were far behind he stopped to take breath, slowly rosined his bow, so that the strings should sound more shrilly, then set off again, by turns lowering and raising his neck, the better to mark time for himself. The noise of the instrument drove away the little birds from afar.

The table was laid under the cart-shed. On it were four sirloins, six chicken fricassees, stewed veal, three legs of mutton, and in the middle a fine roast suckling pig, flanked by four chitterlings with sorrel. At the corners were decanters of brandy. Sweet bottled-cider frothed round the corks, and all the glasses had been filled to the brim with wine beforehand. Large dishes of yellow cream, that trembled with the least shake of the table, had designed on their smooth surface the initials of the newly wedded pair in nonpareil arabesques. A confectioner of

Yvetot had been intrusted with the tarts and sweets. As he had only just set up on the place, he had taken a lot of trouble, and at dessert he himself brought in a set dish that evoked loud cries of wonderment. To begin with, at its base there was a square of blue cardboard, representing a temple with porticoes, colonnades, and stucco statuettes all round, and in the niches constellations of gilt paper stars; then on the second stage was a dungeon of Savoy cake, surrounded by many fortifications in candied angelica, almonds, raisins, and quarters of oranges; and finally, on the upper platform a green field with rocks set in lakes of jam, nutshell boats, and a small Cupid balancing himself in a chocolate swing whose two uprights ended in real roses for balls at the top.

Until night they ate. When any of them were too tired of sitting, they went out for a stroll in the yard, or for a game with corks in the granary, and then returned to table. Some towards the finish went to sleep and snored. But with the coffee everyone woke up. Then they began songs, showed off tricks, raised heavy weights, performed feats with their fingers, then tried lifting carts on their shoulders, made broad jokes, kissed the women. At night when they left, the horses, stuffed up to the nostrils with oats, could hardly be got into the shafts; they kicked, reared, the harness broke, their masters laughed or swore; and all night in the light of the moon along country roads there were runaway carts at full gallop plunging into the ditches, jumping over yard after yard of stones, clambering up the hills, with women leaning out from the tilt to catch hold of the reins.

Those who stayed at the Bertaux spent the night drinking in the kitchen. The children had fallen asleep under the seats.

The bride had begged her father to be spared the usual marriage pleasantries. However, a fishmonger, one of their cousins (who had even brought a pair of soles for his wedding present), began to squirt water from his mouth through the keyhole, when old Rouault came up just in time to stop him, and explain to him that the distinguished position of his son-in-law would not allow of such liberties. The cousin all the same did not give in to these reasons readily. In his heart he accused old Rouault of being proud, and he joined four or five other guests in a corner, who having, through mere chance, been several times running served with the worst helps of meat, also were of opinion they had been badly used, and were whispering about their host, and with covered hints hoping he would ruin himself.

Madame Bovary, senior, had not opened her mouth all day. She had been consulted neither as to the dress of her daughter-in-law nor as to the arrangement of the feast; she went to bed early. Her husband, instead of following her, sent to Saint-Victor for some cigars, and smoked till daybreak, drinking kirsch-punch, a mixture unknown to the company. This added greatly to the consideration in which he was held.

Charles, who was not of a facetious turn, did not shine at the wedding. He answered feebly to the puns, doubles entendres*, compliments, and chaff that it was felt a duty to let off at him as soon as the soup appeared.

The next day, on the other hand, he seemed another man. It was he who might rather have been taken for the virgin of the evening before, whilst the bride gave no sign that revealed anything. The shrewdest did not know what to make of it, and they looked at her when she passed near them with an unbounded concentration of mind. But Charles concealed nothing. He called her "my wife", tutoyed** her, asked for her of everyone, looked for her everywhere, and often he dragged her into the yards, where he could be seen from far between the trees, putting his arm around her waist, and walking half-bending over her, ruffling the chemisette of her bodice with his head.

Two days after the wedding the married pair left. Charles, on account of his patients, could not be away longer. Old Rouault had them driven back in his cart, and himself accompanied them as far as Vassonville. Here he embraced his daughter for the last time, got down, and went his way. When he had gone about a hundred paces he stopped, and as he saw the cart disappearing, its wheels turning in the dust, he gave a deep sigh. Then he remembered his wedding, the old times, the first pregnancy of his wife; he, too, had been very happy the day when he had taken her from her father to his home, and had carried her off on a pillion, trotting through the snow, for it was near Christmas-time, and the country was all white. She held him by one arm, her basket hanging from the other; the wind blew the long lace of her Cauchois headdress so that it sometimes flapped across his mouth, and when he turned his head he saw near him, on his shoulder, her little rosy face, smiling silently under the gold bands of her cap. To warm her hands she put them from time to time in his breast. How long ago it all was! Their son would have been thirty by now. Then he looked back and saw nothing on the road. He felt dreary as an empty house; and tender memories mingling with the sad thoughts in his brain, addled by the

* Double meanings.
** Used the familiar form of address.

GUSTAVE FLAUBERT

fumes of the feast, he felt inclined for a moment to take a turn towards the church. As he was afraid, however, that this sight would make him yet more sad, he went right away home.

Monsieur and Madame Charles arrived at Tostes about six o'clock.

The neighbors came to the windows to see their doctor's new wife.

The old servant presented herself, curtsied to her, apologised for not having dinner ready, and suggested that madame, in the meantime, should look over her house.

Chapter 5

The brick front was just in a line with the street, or rather the road. Behind the door hung a cloak with a small collar, a bridle, and a black leather cap, and on the floor, in a corner, were a pair of leggings, still covered with dry mud. On the right was the one apartment, that was both dining and sitting room. A canary yellow paper, relieved at the top by a garland of pale flowers, was puckered everywhere over the badly stretched canvas; white calico curtains with a red border hung crossways at the length of the window; and on the narrow mantelpiece a clock with a head of Hippocrates shone resplendent between two plate candlesticks under oval shades. On the other side of the passage was Charles's consulting room, a little room about six paces wide, with a table, three chairs, and an office chair. Volumes of the "Dictionary of Medical Science," uncut, but the binding rather the worse for the successive sales through which they had gone, occupied almost along the six shelves of a deal bookcase.

The smell of melted butter penetrated through the walls when he saw patients, just as in the kitchen one could hear the people coughing in the consulting room and recounting their histories.

Then, opening on the yard, where the stable was, came a large dilapidated room with a stove, now used as a wood-house, cellar, and pantry, full of old rubbish, of empty casks, agricultural implements past service, and a mass of dusty things whose use it was impossible to guess.

The garden, longer than wide, ran between two mud walls with espaliered apricots, to a hawthorn hedge that separated it from the field. In the middle was a slate sundial on a brick pedestal; four flower beds with eglantines surrounded symmetrically the more useful kitchen garden bed. Right at the bottom, under the spruce bushes, was a cure in plaster reading his breviary.

Emma went upstairs. The first room was not furnished, but in the second, which was their bedroom, was a mahogany bedstead in an alcove with red drapery. A shell box adorned the chest of drawers, and on the secretary near the window a bouquet of orange blossoms tied with white satin ribbons stood in a bottle. It was a bride's bouquet; it was the other one's. She looked at it. Charles noticed it; he took it and carried it up to the attic, while Emma seated in an arm-chair (they were putting her things down around her) thought of her bridal flowers packed up in a bandbox, and wondered, dreaming, what would be done with them if she were to die.

During the first days she occupied herself in thinking about changes in the house. She took the shades off the candlesticks, had new wallpaper put up, the staircase repainted, and seats made in the garden round the sundial; she even inquired how she could get a basin with a jet fountain and fishes. Finally her husband, knowing that she liked to drive out, picked up a second-hand dogcart, which, with new lamps and splashboard in striped leather, looked almost like a tilbury.

He was happy then, and without a care in the world. A meal together, a walk in the evening on the highroad, a gesture of her hands over her hair, the sight of her straw hat hanging from the window-fastener, and many another thing in which Charles had never dreamed of pleasure, now made up the endless round of his happiness. In bed, in the morning, by her side, on the pillow, he watched the sunlight sinking into the down on her fair cheek, half hidden by the lappets of her night-cap. Seen thus closely, her eyes looked to him enlarged, especially when, on waking up, she opened and shut them rapidly many times. Black in the shade, dark blue in broad daylight, they had, as it were, depths of different colours, that, darker in the centre, grew paler towards the surface of the eye. His own eyes lost themselves in these depths; he saw himself in miniature down to the shoulders, with his handkerchief round his head and the top of his shirt open. He rose. She came to the window to see him off, and stayed leaning on the sill between two pots of geranium, clad in her dressing gown hanging loosely about her. Charles, in the street buckled his spurs, his foot on the mounting stone, while she talked to him from above, picking with her mouth some scrap of flower or leaf that she blew out at him. Then this, eddying, floating, described semicircles in the air like a bird, and was caught before it reached the ground in the ill-groomed mane of the old white mare standing motionless at the door. Charles from horseback threw her a kiss; she answered with a nod; she shut the window, and he set off. And then along the highroad, spreading out its long ribbon of dust, along the deep lanes that the trees bent over as in arbours, along paths where the corn reached to the knees, with the sun on his back and the morning air in his nostrils, his heart full of the joys of the past night, his mind at rest, his flesh at ease, he went on, re-chewing his happiness, like those who after dinner taste again the truffles which they are digesting.

Until now what good had he had of his life? His time at school, when he remained shut up within the high walls, alone, in the midst of companions richer than he or cleverer at their work, who laughed at his accent, who jeered at his clothes, and whose mothers came to the school with cakes in their muffs? Later on, when he studied medicine, and never had his purse full enough to treat some little work-girl who would have become his mistress? Afterwards, he had lived fourteen months with the widow, whose feet in bed were cold as icicles. But now he had for life this beautiful woman whom he adored. For him the universe did not extend beyond the circumference of her petticoat, and he reproached himself with not loving her. He wanted to see her again; he turned back quickly, ran up the stairs with a beating heart. Emma, in her room, was dressing; he came up on tiptoe, kissed her back; she gave a cry.

He could not keep from constantly touching her comb, her ring, her fichu; sometimes he gave her great sounding kisses with all his mouth on her cheeks, or else little kisses in a row all along her bare arm from the tip of her fingers up to her shoulder, and she put him away half-smiling, half-vexed, as you do a child who hangs about you.

Before marriage she thought herself in love; but the happiness that should have followed this love not having come, she must, she thought, have been mistaken. And Emma tried to find out what one meant exactly in life by the words felicity, passion, rapture, that had seemed to her so beautiful in books.

GUSTAVE FLAUBERT

Chapter 6

S he had read "Paul and Virginia," and she had dreamed of the little bamboo-house, the nigger Domingo, the dog Fidele, but above all of the sweet friendship of some dear little brother, who seeks red fruit for you on trees taller than steeples, or who runs barefoot over the sand, bringing you a bird's nest.

When she was thirteen, her father himself took her to town to place her in the convent. They stopped at an inn in the St. Gervais quarter, where, at their supper, they used painted plates that set forth the story of Mademoiselle de la Valliere. The explanatory legends, chipped here and there by the scratching of knives, all glorified religion, the tendernesses of the heart, and the pomps of court.

Far from being bored at first at the convent, she took pleasure in the society of the good sisters, who, to amuse her, took her to the chapel, which one entered from the refectory by a long corridor. She played very little during recreation hours, knew her catechism well, and it was she who always answered Monsieur le Vicaire's difficult questions. Living thus, without ever leaving the warm atmosphere of the classrooms, and amid these pale-faced women wearing rosaries with brass crosses, she was softly lulled by the mystic languor exhaled in the perfumes of the altar, the freshness of the holy water, and the lights of the tapers. Instead of attending to mass, she looked at the pious vignettes with their azure borders in her book, and she loved the sick lamb, the sacred heart pierced with sharp arrows, or the poor Jesus sinking beneath the cross he carries. She tried, by way of mortification, to eat nothing a whole day. She puzzled her head to find some vow to fulfil.

When she went to confession, she invented little sins in order that she might stay there longer, kneeling in the shadow, her hands joined, her face against the grating beneath the whispering of the priest. The comparisons of betrothed, husband, celestial lover, and eternal marriage, that recur in sermons, stirred within her soul depths of unexpected sweetness.

In the evening, before prayers, there was some religious reading in the study. On week-nights it was some abstract of sacred history or the Lectures of the Abbe Frayssinous, and on Sundays passages from the "Genie du Christianisme," as a recreation. How she listened at first to the sonorous lamentations of its romantic melancholies reechoing through the world and eternity! If her childhood had been spent in the shop-parlour of some business quarter, she might perhaps have opened her heart to those lyrical invasions of Nature, which usually come to us only through translation in books. But she knew the country too well; she knew the lowing of cattle, the milking, the ploughs.

Accustomed to calm aspects of life, she turned, on the contrary, to those of excitement. She loved the sea only for the sake of its storms, and the green fields only when broken up by ruins.

She wanted to get some personal profit out of things, and she rejected as useless all that did not contribute to the immediate desires of her heart, being of a temperament more sentimental than artistic, looking for emotions, not landscapes.

At the convent there was an old maid who came for a week each month to mend the linen. Patronized by the clergy, because she belonged to an ancient family of noblemen ruined by the Revolution, she dined in the refectory at the table of the good sisters, and after the meal had a bit of chat with them before going back to her work. The girls often slipped out from the study to go and see her. She knew by heart the love songs of the last century, and sang them in a low voice as she stitched away.

She told stories, gave them news, went errands in the town, and on the sly lent the big girls some novel, that she always carried in the pockets of her apron, and of which the good lady herself swallowed long chapters in the intervals of her work. They were all love, lovers, sweethearts, persecuted ladies fainting in lonely pavilions, postilions killed at every stage, horses ridden to death on every page, sombre forests, heartaches, vows, sobs, tears and kisses, little skiffs by moonlight, nightingales in shady groves, "gentlemen" brave as lions, gentle as lambs, virtuous as no one ever was, always well dressed, and weeping like fountains. For six months, then, Emma, at fifteen years of age, made her hands dirty with books from old lending libraries.

Through Walter Scott, later on, she fell in love with historical events, dreamed of old chests, guard-rooms and minstrels. She would have liked to live in some old manor-house, like those long-waisted chatelaines who, in the shade of pointed arches, spent their days leaning on the stone, chin in hand, watching a cavalier with white plume galloping on his black horse from the distant fields. At this time she had a cult for Mary Stuart and enthusiastic veneration for illustrious or unhappy women. Joan of Arc, Heloise, Agnes Sorel, the beautiful Ferroniere, and Clemence Isaure stood out to her like comets in the dark immensity of heaven, where also were seen, lost in shadow, and all unconnected, St. Louis with his oak, the dying Bayard, some cruelties of Louis XI, a little of St. Bartholomew's Day, the plume of the Bearnais, and always the remembrance of the plates painted in honour of Louis XIV.

In the music class, in the ballads she sang, there was nothing but little angels with golden wings, madonnas, lagunes, gondoliers;-mild compositions that allowed her to catch a glimpse athwart the obscurity of style and the weakness of the music of the attractive phantasmagoria of sentimental realities. Some of her companions brought "keepsakes" given them as new year's gifts to the convent. These had to be hidden; it was quite an undertaking; they were read in the dormitory. Delicately handling the beautiful satin bindings, Emma looked with dazzled eyes at the names of the unknown authors, who had signed their verses for the most part as counts or viscounts.

She trembled as she blew back the tissue paper over the engraving and saw it folded in two and fall gently against the page. Here behind the balustrade of a balcony was a young man in a short cloak, holding in his arms a young girl in a white dress wearing an alms-bag at her belt; or there were nameless portraits of English ladies with fair curls, who looked at you from under their round straw hats with their large clear eyes. Some there were lounging in their carriages, gliding through parks, a greyhound bounding along in front of the equipage driven at a trot by two midget postilions in white breeches. Others, dreaming on sofas with an open letter, gazed at the moon through a slightly open window half draped by a black curtain. The naive ones, a tear on their cheeks, were kissing doves through the bars of a Gothic cage, or, smiling, their heads on one side, were plucking the leaves of a marguerite with their taper fingers, that curved at the tips like peaked shoes. And you, too, were there, Sultans with long pipes reclining beneath arbours in the arms of Bayaderes; Djiaours, Turkish sabres, Greek caps; and you especially, pale landscapes of dithyrambic lands, that often show us at once palm trees and firs, tigers on the right, a lion to the left, Tartar minarets on the horizon; the whole framed by a very neat virgin forest, and with a great perpendicular sunbeam trembling in the water, where, standing out in relief like white excoriations on a steel-grey ground, swans are swimming about.

And the shade of the argand lamp fastened to the wall above Emma's head lighted up all these pictures of the world, that passed before her one by one in the silence of the dormitory, and to the distant noise of some belated carriage rolling over the Boulevards.

When her mother died she cried much the first few days. She had a funeral picture made with the hair of the deceased, and, in a letter sent to the Bertaux full of sad reflections on life, she asked to be buried later on in the same grave. The goodman thought she must be ill, and came to see her. Emma was secretly pleased that she had reached at a first attempt the rare ideal of pale lives, never attained by mediocre hearts. She let herself glide along with Lamartine meanderings, listened to harps on lakes, to all the songs of dying swans, to the falling of the leaves, the pure virgins ascending to heaven, and the voice of the Eternal discoursing down the valleys. She wearied of it, would not confess it, continued from habit, and at last was surprised to feel herself soothed, and with no more sadness at heart than wrinkles on her brow.

The good nuns, who had been so sure of her vocation, perceived with great astonishment that Mademoiselle Rouault seemed to be slipping from them. They had indeed been so lavish to her of prayers, retreats, novenas, and sermons, they had so often preached the respect due to saints and martyrs, and given so much good advice as to the modesty of the body and the salvation of her soul, that she did as tightly reined horses; she pulled up short and the bit slipped from her teeth. This nature, positive in the midst of its enthusiasms, that had loved the church for the sake of the flowers, and music for the words of the songs, and literature for its passional stimulus, rebelled against the mysteries of faith as it grew irritated by discipline, a thing antipathetic to her constitution. When her father took her from school, no one was sorry to see her go. The Lady Superior even thought that she had latterly been somewhat irreverent to the community.

Emma, at home once more, first took pleasure in looking after the servants, then grew disgusted with the country and missed her convent. When Charles came to the Bertaux for the first time, she thought herself quite disillusioned, with nothing more to learn, and nothing more to feel.

But the uneasiness of her new position, or perhaps the disturbance caused by the presence of this man, had sufficed to make her believe that she at last felt that wondrous passion which, till then, like a great bird with rose-coloured wings, hung in the splendour of the skies of poesy; and now she could not think that the calm in which she lived was the happiness she had dreamed.

Chapter 7

She thought, sometimes, that, after all, this was the happiest time of her life—the honeymoon, as people called it. To taste the full sweetness of it, it would have been necessary doubtless to fly to those lands with sonorous names where the days after marriage are full of laziness most suave. In post chaises behind blue silken curtains to ride slowly up steep road, listening to the song of the postilion re-echoed by the mountains, along with the bells of goats and the muffled sound of a waterfall; at sunset on the shores of gulfs to breathe in the perfume of lemon trees; then in the evening on the villa-terraces above, hand in hand to look at the stars, making plans for the future. It seemed to her that certain places on earth must bring happiness, as a plant peculiar to the soil, and that cannot thrive elsewhere. Why could not she lean over balconies in Swiss chalets, or enshrine her melancholy in a Scotch cottage, with a husband dressed in a black velvet coat with long tails, and thin shoes, a pointed hat and frills? Perhaps she would have liked to confide all these things to someone. But how tell an undefinable uneasiness, variable as the clouds, unstable as the winds? Words failed her—the opportunity, the courage.

If Charles had but wished it, if he had guessed it, if his look had but once met her thought, it seemed to her that a sudden plenty would have gone out from her heart, as the fruit falls from a tree when shaken by a hand. But as the intimacy of their life became deeper, the greater became the gulf that separated her from him.

Charles's conversation was commonplace as a street pavement, and everyone's ideas trooped through it in their everyday garb, without exciting emotion, laughter, or thought. He had never had the curiosity, he said, while he lived at Rouen, to go to the theatre to see the actors from Paris. He could neither swim, nor fence, nor shoot, and one day he could not explain some term of horsemanship to her that she had come across in a novel.

A man, on the contrary, should he not know everything, excel in manifold activities, initiate you into the energies of passion, the refinements of life, all mysteries? But this one taught nothing, knew nothing, wished nothing. He thought her happy; and she resented this easy calm, this serene heaviness, the very happiness she gave him.

Sometimes she would draw; and it was great amusement to Charles to stand there bolt upright and watch her bend over her cardboard, with eyes half-closed the better to see her work, or rolling, between her fingers, little bread-pellets. As to the piano, the more quickly her fingers glided over it the more he wondered. She struck the notes with aplomb, and ran from top to bottom of the keyboard without a break. Thus shaken up, the old instrument, whose strings buzzed, could be heard at the other end of the village when the window was open, and often the bailiff's clerk, passing along the highroad bare-headed and in list slippers, stopped to listen, his sheet of paper in his hand.

Emma, on the other hand, knew how to look after her house. She sent the patients' accounts in well-phrased letters that had no suggestion of a bill. When they had a neighbour to dinner on Sundays, she managed to have some tasty dish—piled up pyramids of greengages on vine leaves, served up preserves turned out into plates—and even spoke of buying finger-glasses for dessert. From all this much consideration was extended to Bovary.

Charles finished by rising in his own esteem for possessing such a wife. He showed with pride in the sitting room two small pencil sketches by her that he had had framed in very large frames, and hung up against the wallpaper by long green cords. People returning from mass saw him at his door in his wool-work slippers.

He came home late—at ten o'clock, at midnight sometimes. Then he asked for something to eat, and as the servant had gone to bed, Emma waited on him. He took off his coat to dine more at his ease. He told her, one after the other, the people he had met, the villages where he had been, the prescriptions he had written, and, well pleased with himself, he finished the remainder of the boiled beef and onions, picked pieces off the cheese, munched an apple, emptied his water-bottle, and then went to bed, and lay on his back and snored.

As he had been for a time accustomed to wear nightcaps, his handkerchief would not keep down over his ears, so that his hair in the morning was all tumbled pell-mell about his face and whitened with the feathers of the pillow, whose strings came untied during the night. He always wore thick boots that had two long creases over the instep running obliquely towards the ankle, while the rest of the upper continued in a straight line as if stretched on a wooden foot. He said that "was quite good enough for the country."

His mother approved of his economy, for she came to see him as formerly when there had been some violent row at her place; and yet Madame Bovary senior seemed prejudiced against her daughter-in-law.

She thought "her ways too fine for their position"; the wood, the sugar, and the candles disappeared as "at a grand establishment," and the amount of firing in the kitchen would have been enough for twenty-five courses. She put her linen in order for her in the presses, and taught her to keep an eye on the butcher when he brought the meat. Emma put up with these lessons. Madame Bovary was lavish of them; and the words "daughter" and "mother" were exchanged all day long, accompanied by little quiverings of the lips, each one uttering gentle words in a voice trembling with anger.

In Madame Dubuc's time the old woman felt that she was still the favorite; but now the love of Charles for Emma seemed to her a desertion from her tenderness, an encroachment upon what was hers, and she watched her son's happiness in sad silence, as a ruined man looks through the windows at people dining in his old house. She recalled to him as remembrances her troubles and her sacrifices, and, comparing these with Emma's negligence, came to the conclusion that it was not reasonable to adore her so exclusively.

Charles knew not what to answer: he respected his mother, and he loved his wife infinitely; he considered the judgment of the one infallible, and yet he thought the conduct of the other irreproachable. When Madam Bovary had gone, he tried timidly and in the same terms to hazard one or two of the more anodyne observations he had heard from his mamma. Emma proved to him with a word that he was mistaken, and sent him off to his patients.

And yet, in accord with theories she believed right, she wanted to make herself in love with him. By moonlight in the garden she recited all the passionate rhymes she knew by heart, and, sighing, sang to him many melancholy adagios; but she found herself as calm after as before, and Charles seemed no more amorous and no more moved.

When she had thus for a while struck the flint on her heart without getting a spark, incapable, moreover, of understanding what she did not experience as of believing anything that did not present itself in conventional forms, she persuaded herself without difficulty that Charles's passion was nothing very exorbitant. His outbursts became regular; he embraced her at certain fixed times. It was one habit among other habits, and, like a dessert, looked forward to after the monotony of dinner.

A gamekeeper, cured by the doctor of inflammation of the lungs, had given madame a little Italian greyhound; she took her out walking, for she went out sometimes in order to be alone for a moment, and not to see before her eyes the eternal garden and the dusty road. She went as far as the beeches of Banneville, near the deserted pavilion which forms an angle of the wall on the side of the country. Amidst the vegetation of the ditch there are long reeds with leaves that cut you.

She began by looking round her to see if nothing had changed since last she had been there. She found again in the same places the foxgloves and wallflowers, the beds of nettles growing round the big stones, and the patches of lichen along the three windows, whose shutters, always closed, were rotting away on their rusty iron bars. Her thoughts, aimless at first, wandered at random, like her greyhound, who ran round and round in the fields, yelping after the yellow butterflies, chasing the shrew-mice, or nibbling the poppies on the edge of a cornfield.

Then gradually her ideas took definite shape, and, sitting on the grass that she dug up with little prods of her sunshade, Emma repeated to herself, "Good heavens! Why did I marry?"

She asked herself if by some other chance combination it would have not been possible to meet another man; and she tried to imagine what would have been these unrealised events, this different life, this unknown husband. All, surely, could not be like this one. He might have been handsome, witty, distinguished, attractive, such as, no doubt, her old companions of the convent had married. What were they doing now? In town, with the noise of the streets, the buzz of the theatres and the lights of the ballroom, they were living lives where the heart expands, the senses bourgeon out. But she—her life was cold as a garret whose dormer window looks on the north, and ennui, the silent spider, was weaving its web in the darkness in every corner of her heart.

She recalled the prize days, when she mounted the platform to receive her little crowns, with her hair in long plaits. In her white frock and open prunella shoes she had a pretty way, and when she went back to her seat, the gentlemen bent over her to congratulate her; the courtyard was full of carriages; farewells were called to her through their windows; the music master with his violin case bowed in passing by. How far all of this! How far away! She called Djali, took her between her knees, and smoothed the long delicate head, saying, "Come, kiss mistress; you have no troubles."

Then noting the melancholy face of the graceful animal, who yawned slowly, she softened, and comparing her to herself, spoke to her aloud as to somebody in trouble whom one is consoling.

Occasionally there came gusts of winds, breezes from the sea rolling in one sweep over the whole plateau of the Caux country, which

GUSTAVE FLAUBERT

brought even to these fields a salt freshness. The rushes, close to the ground, whistled; the branches trembled in a swift rustling, while their summits, ceaselessly swaying, kept up a deep murmur. Emma drew her shawl round her shoulders and rose.

In the avenue a green light dimmed by the leaves lit up the short moss that crackled softly beneath her feet. The sun was setting; the sky showed red between the branches, and the trunks of the trees, uniform, and planted in a straight line, seemed a brown colonnade standing out against a background of gold. A fear took hold of her; she called Djali, and hurriedly returned to Tostes by the high road, threw herself into an armchair, and for the rest of the evening did not speak.

But towards the end of September something extraordinary fell upon her life; she was invited by the Marquis d'Andervilliers to Vaubyessard.

Secretary of State under the Restoration, the Marquis, anxious to re-enter political life, set about preparing for his candidature to the Chamber of Deputies long beforehand. In the winter he distributed a great deal of wood, and in the Conseil General always enthusiastically demanded new roads for his arrondissement. During the dog-days he had suffered from an abscess, which Charles had cured as if by miracle by giving a timely little touch with the lancet. The steward sent to Tostes to pay for the operation reported in the evening that he had seen some superb cherries in the doctor's little garden. Now cherry trees did not thrive at Vaubyessard; the Marquis asked Bovary for some slips; made it his business to thank his personally; saw Emma; thought she had a pretty figure, and that she did not bow like a peasant; so that he did not think he was going beyond the bounds of condescension, nor, on the other hand, making a mistake, in inviting the young couple.

On Wednesday at three o'clock, Monsieur and Madame Bovary, seated in their dog-cart, set out for Vaubyessard, with a great trunk strapped on behind and a bonnet-box in front of the apron. Besides these Charles held a bandbox between his knees.

They arrived at nightfall, just as the lamps in the park were being lit to show the way for the carriages.

Chapter 8

The chateau, a modern building in Italian style, with two projecting wings and three flights of steps, lay at the foot of an immense greensward, on which some cows were grazing among groups of large trees set out at regular intervals, while large beds of arbutus, rhododendron, syringas, and guelder roses bulged out their irregular clusters of green along the curve of the gravel path. A river flowed under a bridge; through the mist one could distinguish buildings with thatched roofs scattered over the field bordered by two gently sloping, well timbered hillocks, and in the background amid the trees rose in two parallel lines the coach houses and stables, all that was left of the ruined old chateau.

Charles's dog-cart pulled up before the middle flight of steps; servants appeared; the Marquis came forward, and, offering his arm to the doctor's wife, conducted her to the vestibule.

It was paved with marble slabs, was very lofty, and the sound of footsteps and that of voices re-echoed through it as in a church.

Opposite rose a straight staircase, and on the left a gallery overlooking the garden led to the billiard room, through whose door one could hear the click of the ivory balls. As she crossed it to go to the drawing room, Emma saw standing round the table men with grave faces, their chins resting on high cravats. They all wore orders, and smiled silently as they made their strokes.

On the dark wainscoting of the walls large gold frames bore at the bottom names written in black letters. She read: "Jean-Antoine d'Andervilliers d'Yvervonbille, Count de la Vaubyessard and Baron de la Fresnay, killed at the battle of Coutras on the 20th of October, 1587." And on another: "Jean-Antoine-Henry-Guy d'Andervilliers de la Vaubyessard, Admiral of France and Chevalier of the Order of St. Michael, wounded at the battle of the Hougue-Saint-Vaast on the 29th of May, 1692; died at Vaubyessard on the 23rd of January 1693." One could hardly make out those that followed, for the light of the lamps lowered over the green cloth threw a dim shadow round the room. Burnishing the horizontal pictures, it broke up against these in delicate lines where there were cracks in the varnish, and from all these great black squares framed in with gold stood out here and there some lighter portion of the painting—a pale brow, two eyes that looked at you, perukes flowing over and powdering red-coated shoulders, or the buckle of a garter above a well-rounded calf.

GUSTAVE FLAUBERT

The Marquis opened the drawing room door; one of the ladies (the Marchioness herself) came to meet Emma. She made her sit down by her on an ottoman, and began talking to her as amicably as if she had known her a long time. She was a woman of about forty, with fine shoulders, a hook nose, a drawling voice, and on this evening she wore over her brown hair a simple guipure fichu that fell in a point at the back. A fair young woman sat in a high-backed chair in a corner; and gentlemen with flowers in their buttonholes were talking to ladies round the fire.

At seven dinner was served. The men, who were in the majority, sat down at the first table in the vestibule; the ladies at the second in the dining room with the Marquis and Marchioness.

Emma, on entering, felt herself wrapped round by the warm air, a blending of the perfume of flowers and of the fine linen, of the fumes of the viands, and the odour of the truffles. The silver dish covers reflected the lighted wax candles in the candelabra, the cut crystal covered with light steam reflected from one to the other pale rays; bouquets were placed in a row the whole length of the table; and in the large-bordered plates each napkin, arranged after the fashion of a bishop's mitre, held between its two gaping folds a small oval shaped roll. The red claws of lobsters hung over the dishes; rich fruit in open baskets was piled up on moss; there were quails in their plumage; smoke was rising; and in silk stockings, knee-breeches, white cravat, and frilled shirt, the steward, grave as a judge, offering ready carved dishes between the shoulders of the guests, with a touch of the spoon gave you the piece chosen. On the large stove of porcelain inlaid with copper baguettes the statue of a woman, draped to the chin, gazed motionless on the room full of life.

Madame Bovary noticed that many ladies had not put their gloves in their glasses.

But at the upper end of the table, alone amongst all these women, bent over his full plate, and his napkin tied round his neck like a child, an old man sat eating, letting drops of gravy drip from his mouth. His eyes were bloodshot, and he wore a little queue tied with black ribbon. He was the Marquis's father-in-law, the old Duke de Laverdiere, once on a time favourite of the Count d'Artois, in the days of the Vaudreuil hunting-parties at the Marquis de Conflans', and had been, it was said, the lover of Queen Marie Antoinette, between Monsieur de Coigny and Monsieur de Lauzun. He had lived a life of noisy debauch, full of duels, bets, elopements; he had squandered his fortune and frightened all his family. A servant behind his chair named aloud to him in his ear the dishes that he pointed to stammering, and constantly Emma's eyes turned involuntarily to this old man with hanging lips, as to something extraordinary. He had lived at court and slept in the bed of queens! Iced champagne was poured out. Emma shivered all over as she felt it cold in her mouth. She had never seen pomegranates nor tasted pineapples. The powdered sugar even seemed to her whiter and finer than elsewhere.

The ladies afterwards went to their rooms to prepare for the ball.

Emma made her toilet with the fastidious care of an actress on her debut. She did her hair according to the directions of the hairdresser, and put on the barege dress spread out upon the bed.

Charles's trousers were tight across the belly.

"My trouser-straps will be rather awkward for dancing," he said.

"Dancing?" repeated Emma.

"Yes!"

"Why, you must be mad! They would make fun of you; keep your place. Besides, it is more becoming for a doctor," she added.

Charles was silent. He walked up and down waiting for Emma to finish dressing.

He saw her from behind in the glass between two lights. Her black eyes seemed blacker than ever. Her hair, undulating towards the ears, shone with a blue lustre; a rose in her chignon trembled on its mobile stalk, with artificial dewdrops on the tip of the leaves. She wore a gown of pale saffron trimmed with three bouquets of pompon roses mixed with green.

Charles came and kissed her on her shoulder.

"Let me alone!" she said; "you are tumbling me."

One could hear the flourish of the violin and the notes of a horn. She went downstairs restraining herself from running.

Dancing had begun. Guests were arriving. There was some crushing. She sat down on a form near the door.

The quadrille over, the floor was occupied by groups of men standing up and talking and servants in livery bearing large trays. Along the line of seated women painted fans were fluttering, bouquets half hid smiling faces, and gold stoppered scent-bottles were turned in partly-closed hands, whose white gloves outlined the nails and tightened on the flesh at the wrists. Lace trimmings, diamond brooches, medallion bracelets trembled on bodices, gleamed on breasts, clinked on bare arms.

The hair, well-smoothed over the temples and knotted at the nape, bore crowns, or bunches, or sprays of mytosotis, jasmine, pomegranate blossoms, ears of corn, and corn-flowers. Calmly seated in their places, mothers with forbidding countenances were wearing red turbans.

Emma's heart beat rather faster when, her partner holding her by the tips of the fingers, she took her place in a line with the dancers, and waited for the first note to start. But her emotion soon vanished, and, swaying to the rhythm of the orchestra, she glided forward with slight movements of the neck. A smile rose to her lips at certain delicate phrases of the violin, that sometimes played alone while the other instruments were silent; one could hear the clear clink of the louis d'or that were being thrown down upon the card tables in the next room; then all struck again, the cornet-a-piston uttered its sonorous note, feet marked time, skirts swelled and rustled, hands touched and parted; the same eyes falling before you met yours again.

A few men (some fifteen or so), of twenty-five to forty, scattered here and there among the dancers or talking at the doorways, distinguished themselves from the crowd by a certain air of breeding, whatever their differences in age, dress, or face.

Their clothes, better made, seemed of finer cloth, and their hair, brought forward in curls towards the temples, glossy with more delicate pomades. They had the complexion of wealth—that clear complexion that is heightened by the pallor of porcelain, the shimmer of satin, the veneer of old furniture, and that an ordered regimen of exquisite nurture maintains at its best. Their necks moved easily in their low cravats, their long whiskers fell over their turned-down collars, they wiped their lips upon handkerchiefs with embroidered initials that gave forth a subtle perfume. Those who were beginning to grow old had an air of youth, while there was something mature in the faces of the young. In their unconcerned looks was the calm of passions daily satiated, and through all their gentleness of manner pierced that peculiar brutality, the result of a command of half-easy things, in which force is exercised and vanity amused—the management of thoroughbred horses and the society of loose women.

A few steps from Emma a gentleman in a blue coat was talking of Italy with a pale young woman wearing a parure of pearls.

They were praising the breadth of the columns of St. Peter's, Tivoly, Vesuvius, Castellamare, and Cassines, the roses of Genoa, the Coliseum by moonlight. With her other ear Emma was listening to a conversation full of words she did not understand. A circle gathered round a very young man who the week before had beaten "Miss Arabella" and "Romolus," and won two thousand louis jumping a ditch in England. One complained that his racehorses were growing fat; another of the printers' errors that had disfigured the name of his horse.

The atmosphere of the ball was heavy; the lamps were growing dim.

Guests were flocking to the billiard room. A servant got upon a chair and broke the window-panes. At the crash of the glass Madame Bovary turned her head and saw in the garden the faces of peasants pressed against the window looking in at them. Then the memory of the Bertaux came back to her. She saw the farm again, the muddy pond, her father in a blouse under the apple trees, and she saw herself again as formerly, skimming with her finger the cream off the milk-pans in the dairy. But in the refulgence of the present hour her past life, so distinct until then, faded away completely, and she almost doubted having lived it. She was there; beyond the ball was only shadow overspreading all the rest. She was just eating a maraschino ice that she held with her left hand in a silver-gilt cup, her eyes half-closed, and the spoon between her teeth.

A lady near her dropped her fan. A gentlemen was passing.

"Would you be so good," said the lady, "as to pick up my fan that has fallen behind the sofa?"

The gentleman bowed, and as he moved to stretch out his arm, Emma saw the hand of a young woman throw something white, folded in a triangle, into his hat. The gentleman, picking up the fan, offered it to the lady respectfully; she thanked him with an inclination of the head, and began smelling her bouquet.

After supper, where were plenty of Spanish and Rhine wines, soups a la bisque and au lait d'amandes*, puddings a la Trafalgar, and all sorts of cold meats with jellies that trembled in the dishes, the carriages one after the other began to drive off. Raising the corners of the muslin curtain, one could see the light of their lanterns glimmering through the darkness. The seats began to empty, some card-players were still left; the musicians were cooling the tips of their fingers on their tongues. Charles was half asleep, his back propped against a door.

At three o'clock the cotillion began. Emma did not know how to waltz. Everyone was waltzing, Mademoiselle d'Andervilliers herself and the Marquis; only the guests staying at the castle were still there, about a dozen persons.

---

* With almond milk

One of the waltzers, however, who was familiarly called Viscount, and whose low cut waistcoat seemed moulded to his chest, came a second time to ask Madame Bovary to dance, assuring her that he would guide her, and that she would get through it very well.

They began slowly, then went more rapidly. They turned; all around them was turning—the lamps, the furniture, the wainscoting, the floor, like a disc on a pivot. On passing near the doors the bottom of Emma's dress caught against his trousers.

Their legs commingled; he looked down at her; she raised her eyes to his. A torpor seized her; she stopped. They started again, and with a more rapid movement; the Viscount, dragging her along disappeared with her to the end of the gallery, where panting, she almost fell, and for a moment rested her head upon his breast. And then, still turning, but more slowly, he guided her back to her seat. She leaned back against the wall and covered her eyes with her hands.

When she opened them again, in the middle of the drawing room three waltzers were kneeling before a lady sitting on a stool.

She chose the Viscount, and the violin struck up once more.

Everyone looked at them. They passed and re-passed, she with rigid body, her chin bent down, and he always in the same pose, his figure curved, his elbow rounded, his chin thrown forward. That woman knew how to waltz! They kept up a long time, and tired out all the others.

Then they talked a few moments longer, and after the goodnights, or rather good mornings, the guests of the chateau retired to bed.

Charles dragged himself up by the balusters. His "knees were going up into his body." He had spent five consecutive hours standing bolt upright at the card tables, watching them play whist, without understanding anything about it, and it was with a deep sigh of relief that he pulled off his boots.

Emma threw a shawl over her shoulders, opened the window, and leant out.

The night was dark; some drops of rain were falling. She breathed in the damp wind that refreshed her eyelids. The music of the ball was still murmuring in her ears. And she tried to keep herself awake in order to prolong the illusion of this luxurious life that she would soon have to give up.

Day began to break. She looked long at the windows of the chateau, trying to guess which were the rooms of all those she had noticed the evening before. She would fain have known their lives, have penetrated, blended with them. But she was shivering with cold. She undressed, and cowered down between the sheets against Charles, who was asleep.

There were a great many people to luncheon. The repast lasted ten minutes; no liqueurs were served, which astonished the doctor.

Next, Mademoiselle d'Andervilliers collected some pieces of roll in a small basket to take them to the swans on the ornamental waters, and they went to walk in the hot-houses, where strange plants, bristling with hairs, rose in pyramids under hanging vases, whence, as from over-filled nests of serpents, fell long green cords interlacing. The orangery, which was at the other end, led by a covered way to the outhouses of the chateau. The Marquis, to amuse the young woman, took her to see the stables.

Above the basket-shaped racks porcelain slabs bore the names of the horses in black letters. Each animal in its stall whisked its tail when anyone went near and said "Tchk! tchk!" The boards of the harness room shone like the flooring of a drawing room. The carriage harness was piled up in the middle against two twisted columns, and the bits, the whips, the spurs, the curbs, were ranged in a line all along the wall.

Charles, meanwhile, went to ask a groom to put his horse to. The dog-cart was brought to the foot of the steps, and, all the parcels being crammed in, the Bovarys paid their respects to the Marquis and Marchioness and set out again for Tostes.

Emma watched the turning wheels in silence. Charles, on the extreme edge of the seat, held the reins with his two arms wide apart, and the little horse ambled along in the shafts that were too big for him. The loose reins hanging over his crupper were wet with foam, and the box fastened on behind the chaise gave great regular bumps against it.

They were on the heights of Thibourville when suddenly some horsemen with cigars between their lips passed laughing. Emma thought she recognized the Viscount, turned back, and caught on the horizon only the movement of the heads rising or falling with the unequal cadence of the trot or gallop.

A mile farther on they had to stop to mend with some string the traces that had broken.

But Charles, giving a last look to the harness, saw something on the ground between his horse's legs, and he picked up a cigar-case with a green silk border and beblazoned in the centre like the door of a carriage.

"There are even two cigars in it," said he; "they'll do for this evening after dinner."

"Why, do you smoke?" she asked.

"Sometimes, when I get a chance."

He put his find in his pocket and whipped up the nag.

When they reached home the dinner was not ready. Madame lost her temper. Nastasie answered rudely.

"Leave the room!" said Emma. "You are forgetting yourself. I give you warning."

For dinner there was onion soup and a piece of veal with sorrel.

Charles, seated opposite Emma, rubbed his hands gleefully.

"How good it is to be at home again!"

Nastasie could be heard crying. He was rather fond of the poor girl. She had formerly, during the wearisome time of his widowhood, kept him company many an evening. She had been his first patient, his oldest acquaintance in the place.

"Have you given her warning for good?" he asked at last.

"Yes. Who is to prevent me?" she replied.

Then they warmed themselves in the kitchen while their room was being made ready. Charles began to smoke. He smoked with lips protruding, spitting every moment, recoiling at every puff.

"You'll make yourself ill," she said scornfully.

He put down his cigar and ran to swallow a glass of cold water at the pump. Emma seizing hold of the cigar case threw it quickly to the back of the cupboard.

The next day was a long one. She walked about her little garden, up and down the same walks, stopping before the beds, before the espalier, before the plaster curate, looking with amazement at all these things of once-on-a-time that she knew so well. How far off the ball seemed already! What was it that thus set so far asunder the morning of the day before yesterday and the evening of to-day? Her journey to Vaubyessard had made a hole in her life, like one of those great crevices that a storm will sometimes make in one night in mountains. Still she was resigned. She devoutly put away in her drawers her beautiful dress, down to the satin shoes whose soles were yellowed with the slippery wax of the dancing floor. Her heart was like these. In its friction against wealth something had come over it that could not be effaced.

The memory of this ball, then, became an occupation for Emma.

Whenever the Wednesday came round she said to herself as she awoke, "Ah! I was there a week—a fortnight—three weeks ago."

And little by little the faces grew confused in her remembrance.

She forgot the tune of the quadrilles; she no longer saw the liveries and appointments so distinctly; some details escaped her, but the regret remained with her.

Chapter 9

Often when Charles was out she took from the cupboard, between the folds of the linen where she had left it, the green silk cigar case. She looked at it, opened it, and even smelt the odour of the lining—a mixture of verbena and tobacco. Whose was it? The Viscount's? Perhaps it was a present from his mistress. It had been embroidered on some rosewood frame, a pretty little thing, hidden from all eyes, that had occupied many hours, and over which had fallen the soft curls of the pensive worker. A breath of love had passed over the stitches on the canvas; each prick of the needle had fixed there a hope or a memory, and all those interwoven threads of silk were but the continuity of the same silent passion. And then one morning the Viscount had taken it away with him. Of what had they spoken when it lay upon the wide-mantelled chimneys between flower-vases and Pompadour clocks? She was at Tostes; he was at Paris now, far away! What was this Paris like? What a vague name! She repeated it in a low voice, for the mere pleasure of it; it rang in her ears like a great cathedral bell; it shone before her eyes, even on the labels of her pomade-pots.

At night, when the carriers passed under her windows in their carts singing the "Marjolaine," she awoke, and listened to the noise of the iron-bound wheels, which, as they gained the country road, was soon deadened by the soil. "They will be there to-morrow!" she said to herself.

And she followed them in thought up and down the hills, traversing villages, gliding along the highroads by the light of the stars. At the end of some indefinite distance there was always a confused spot, into which her dream died.

She bought a plan of Paris, and with the tip of her finger on the map she walked about the capital. She went up the boulevards, stopping at every turning, between the lines of the streets, in front of the white squares that represented the houses. At last she would close the lids of her weary eyes, and see in the darkness the gas jets flaring in the wind and the steps of carriages lowered with much noise before the peristyles of theatres.

She took in "La Corbeille," a lady's journal, and the "Sylphe des Salons." She devoured, without skipping a word, all the accounts of first nights, races, and soirees, took interest in the debut of a singer, in the opening of a new shop. She knew the latest fashions, the addresses of the best tailors, the days of the Bois and the Opera. In Eugene Sue she studied descriptions of furniture; she read Balzac and George Sand, seeking in them imaginary satisfaction for her own desires. Even at table she had her book by her, and turned over the pages while Charles ate and talked to her. The memory of the Viscount always returned as she read. Between him and the imaginary personages she made comparisons. But the circle of which he was the centre gradually widened round him, and the aureole that he bore, fading from his form, broadened out beyond, lighting up her other dreams.

Paris, more vague than the ocean, glimmered before Emma's eyes in an atmosphere of vermilion. The many lives that stirred amid this tumult were, however, divided into parts, classed as distinct pictures. Emma perceived only two or three that hid from her all the rest, and in themselves represented all humanity. The world of ambassadors moved over polished floors in drawing rooms lined with mirrors, round oval tables covered with velvet and gold-fringed cloths. There were dresses with trains, deep mysteries, anguish hidden beneath smiles. Then came the society of the duchesses; all were pale; all got up at four o'clock; the women, poor angels, wore English point on their petticoats; and the men, unappreciated geniuses under a frivolous outward seeming, rode horses to death at pleasure parties, spent the summer season at Baden, and towards the forties married heiresses. In the private rooms of restaurants, where one sups after midnight by the light of wax candles, laughed the motley crowd of men of letters and actresses. They were prodigal as kings, full of ideal, ambitious, fantastic frenzy. This was an existence outside that of all others, between heaven and earth, in the midst of storms, having something of the sublime. For the rest of the world it was lost, with no particular place and as if non-existent. The nearer things were, moreover, the more her thoughts turned away from them. All her immediate surroundings, the wearisome country, the middle-class imbeciles, the mediocrity of existence, seemed to her exceptional, a peculiar chance that had caught hold of her, while beyond stretched, as far as eye could see, an immense land of joys and passions. She confused in her desire the sensualities of luxury with the delights of the heart, elegance of manners with delicacy of sentiment. Did not love, like Indian plants, need a special soil, a particular temperature? Signs by moonlight, long embraces, tears flowing over yielded hands, all the fevers of the flesh and the languors of tenderness could not be separated from the balconies of great castles full of indolence, from boudoirs with silken curtains and thick carpets, well-filled flower-stands, a bed on a raised dias, nor from the flashing of precious stones and the shoulder-knots of liveries.

The lad from the posting house who came to groom the mare every morning passed through the passage with his heavy wooden shoes; there were holes in his blouse; his feet were bare in list slippers. And this was the groom in knee-britches with whom she had to be content! His work done, he did not come back again all day, for Charles on his return put up his horse himself, unsaddled him and put on the halter, while the servant-girl brought a bundle of straw and threw it as best she could into the manger.

To replace Nastasie (who left Tostes shedding torrents of tears) Emma took into her service a young girl of fourteen, an orphan with a sweet face. She forbade her wearing cotton caps, taught her to address her in the third person, to bring a glass of water on a plate, to knock before coming into a room, to iron, starch, and to dress her—wanted to make a lady's-maid of her. The new servant obeyed without a murmur, so as not to be sent away; and as madame usually left the key in the sideboard, Felicite every evening took a small supply of sugar that she ate alone in her bed after she had said her prayers.

Sometimes in the afternoon she went to chat with the postilions.

Madame was in her room upstairs. She wore an open dressing gown that showed between the shawl facings of her bodice a pleated chamisette with three gold buttons. Her belt was a corded girdle with great tassels, and her small garnet coloured slippers had a large knot of ribbon that fell over her instep. She had bought herself a blotting book, writing case, pen-holder, and envelopes, although she had no one to write to; she dusted her what-not, looked at herself in the glass, picked up a book, and then, dreaming between the lines, let it drop on her knees. She longed to travel or to go back to her convent. She wished at the same time to die and to live in Paris.

Charles in snow and rain trotted across country. He ate omelettes on farmhouse tables, poked his arm into damp beds, received the tepid spurt of blood-lettings in his face, listened to death-rattles, examined basins, turned over a good deal of dirty linen; but every evening he found a blazing fire, his dinner ready, easy-chairs, and a well-dressed woman, charming with an odour of freshness, though no one could say whence the perfume came, or if it were not her skin that made odorous her chemise.

She charmed him by numerous attentions; now it was some new way of arranging paper sconces for the candles, a flounce that she altered on her gown, or an extraordinary name for some very simple dish that the servant had spoilt, but that Charles swallowed with pleasure to the last mouthful. At Rouen she saw some ladies who wore a bunch of charms on the watch-chains; she bought some charms. She wanted for her mantelpiece two large blue glass vases, and some time after an ivory necessaire with a silver-gilt thimble. The less Charles understood these refinements the more they seduced him. They added something to the pleasure of the senses and to the comfort of his fireside. It was like a golden dust sanding all along the narrow path of his life.

He was well, looked well; his reputation was firmly established.

The country-folk loved him because he was not proud. He petted the children, never went to the public house, and, moreover, his morals inspired confidence. He was specially successful with catarrhs and chest complaints. Being much afraid of killing his patients, Charles, in fact only prescribed sedatives, from time to time and emetic, a footbath, or leeches. It was not that he was afraid of surgery; he bled people copiously like horses, and for the taking out of teeth he had the "devil's own wrist."

Finally, to keep up with the times, he took in "La Ruche Medicale," a new journal whose prospectus had been sent him. He read it a little after dinner, but in about five minutes the warmth of the room added to the effect of his dinner sent him to sleep; and he sat there, his chin on his two hands and his hair spreading like a mane to the foot of the lamp. Emma looked at him and shrugged her shoulders. Why, at least, was not her husband one of those men of taciturn passions who work at their books all night, and at last, when about sixty, the age of rheumatism sets in, wear a string of orders on their ill-fitting black coat? She could have wished this name of Bovary, which was hers, had been illustrious, to see it displayed at the booksellers', repeated in the newspapers, known to all France. But Charles had no ambition.

An Yvetot doctor whom he had lately met in consultation had somewhat humiliated him at the very bedside of the patient, before the assembled relatives. When, in the evening, Charles told her this anecdote, Emma inveighed loudly against his colleague. Charles was much touched. He kissed her forehead with a tear in his eyes. But she was angered with shame; she felt a wild desire to strike him; she went to open the window in the passage and breathed in the fresh air to calm herself.

"What a man! What a man!" she said in a low voice, biting her lips.

Besides, she was becoming more irritated with him. As he grew older his manner grew heavier; at dessert he cut the corks of the empty bottles; after eating he cleaned his teeth with his tongue; in taking soup he made a gurgling noise with every spoonful; and, as he was getting fatter, the puffed-out cheeks seemed to push the eyes, always small, up to the temples.

Sometimes Emma tucked the red borders of his under-vest unto his waistcoat, rearranged his cravat, and threw away the dirty gloves he was going to put on; and this was not, as he fancied, for himself; it was for herself, by a diffusion of egotism, of nervous irritation. Sometimes, too, she told him of what she had read, such as a passage in a novel, of a new play, or an anecdote of the "upper ten" that she had seen in a feuilleton; for, after all, Charles was something, an ever-open ear, and ever-ready approbation. She confided many a thing to her greyhound. She would have done so to the logs in the fireplace or to the pendulum of the clock.

At the bottom of her heart, however, she was waiting for something to happen. Like shipwrecked sailors, she turned despairing eyes upon the solitude of her life, seeking afar off some white sail in the mists of the horizon. She did not know what this chance would be, what wind would bring it her, towards what shore it would drive her, if it would be a shallop or a three-decker, laden with anguish or full of bliss to the portholes. But each morning, as she awoke, she hoped it would come that day; she listened to every sound, sprang up with a start, wondered that it did not come; then at sunset, always more saddened, she longed for the morrow.

Spring came round. With the first warm weather, when the pear trees began to blossom, she suffered from dyspnoea.

From the beginning of July she counted how many weeks there were to October, thinking that perhaps the Marquis d'Andervilliers would give another ball at Vaubyessard. But all September passed without letters or visits.

After the ennui of this disappointment her heart once more remained empty, and then the same series of days recommenced. So now they would thus follow one another, always the same, immovable, and bringing nothing. Other lives, however flat, had at least the chance of some event. One adventure sometimes brought with it infinite consequences and the scene changed. But nothing happened to her; God had willed it so! The future was a dark corridor, with its door at the end shut fast.

She gave up music. What was the good of playing? Who would hear her? Since she could never, in a velvet gown with short sleeves, striking with her light fingers the ivory keys of an Erard at a concert, feel the murmur of ecstasy envelop her like a breeze, it was not worth while boring herself with practicing. Her drawing cardboard and her embroidery she left in the cupboard. What was the good? What was the good? Sewing irritated her. "I have read everything," she said to herself. And she sat there making the tongs red-hot, or looked at the rain falling.

How sad she was on Sundays when vespers sounded! She listened with dull attention to each stroke of the cracked bell. A cat slowly walking over some roof put up his back in the pale rays of the sun. The wind on the highroad blew up clouds of dust. Afar off a dog sometimes howled; and the bell, keeping time, continued its monotonous ringing that died away over the fields.

But the people came out from church. The women in waxed clogs, the peasants in new blouses, the little bare-headed children skipping along in front of them, all were going home. And till nightfall, five or six men, always the same, stayed playing at corks in front of the large door of the inn.

The winter was severe. The windows every morning were covered with rime, and the light shining through them, dim as through ground-glass, sometimes did not change the whole day long. At four o'clock the lamp had to be lighted.

On fine days she went down into the garden. The dew had left on the cabbages a silver lace with long transparent threads spreading from one to the other. No birds were to be heard; everything seemed asleep, the espalier covered with straw, and the vine, like a great sick serpent under the coping of the wall, along which, on drawing near, one saw the many-footed woodlice crawling. Under the spruce by the hedgerow, the curie in the three-cornered hat reading his breviary had lost his right foot, and the very plaster, scaling off with the frost, had left white scabs on his face.

Then she went up again, shut her door, put on coals, and fainting with the heat of the hearth, felt her boredom weigh more heavily than ever. She would have liked to go down and talk to the servant, but a sense of shame restrained her.

Every day at the same time the schoolmaster in a black skullcap opened the shutters of his house, and the rural policeman, wearing his sabre over his blouse, passed by. Night and morning the post-horses, three by three, crossed the street to water at the pond. From time to time the bell of a public house door rang, and when it was windy one could hear the little brass basins that served as signs for the hairdresser's shop creaking on their two rods. This shop had as decoration an old engraving of a fashion-plate stuck against a windowpane and the wax bust of a woman with yellow hair. He, too, the hairdresser, lamented his wasted calling, his hopeless future, and dreaming of some shop in a big town—at Rouen, for example, overlooking the harbour, near the theatre—he walked up and down all day from the mairie to the church, sombre and waiting for customers. When Madame Bovary looked up, she always saw him there, like a sentinel on duty, with his skullcap over his ears and his vest of lasting.

Sometimes in the afternoon outside the window of her room, the head of a man appeared, a swarthy head with black whiskers, smiling slowly, with a broad, gentle smile that showed his white teeth. A waltz immediately began and on the organ, in a little drawing room, dancers the size of a finger, women in pink turbans, Tyrolians in jackets, monkeys in frock coats, gentlemen in knee-breeches, turned and turned between the sofas, the consoles, multiplied in the bits of looking glass held together at their corners by a piece of gold paper. The man turned his handle, looking to the right and left, and up at the windows. Now and again, while he shot out a long squirt of brown saliva against the milestone, with his knee raised his instrument, whose hard straps tired his shoulder; and now, doleful and drawling, or gay and hurried, the music escaped from the box, droning through a curtain of pink taffeta under a brass claw in arabesque. They were airs played in other places at the theatres, sung in drawing rooms, danced to at night under lighted lustres, echoes of the world that reached even to Emma. Endless sarabands ran through her head, and, like an Indian dancing girl on the flowers of a carpet, her thoughts leapt with the notes, swung from dream to dream, from sadness to sadness. When the man had caught some coppers in his cap, he drew down an old cover of blue cloth, hitched his organ on to his back, and went off with a heavy tread. She watched him going.

But it was above all the meal-times that were unbearable to her, in this small room on the ground floor, with its smoking stove, its creaking door, the walls that sweated, the damp flags; all the bitterness in life seemed served up on her plate, and with smoke of the boiled beef there rose from her secret soul whiffs of sickliness. Charles was a slow eater; she played with a few nuts, or, leaning on her elbow, amused herself with drawing lines along the oilcloth table cover with the point of her knife.

She now let everything in her household take care of itself, and Madame Bovary senior, when she came to spend part of Lent at

Tostes, was much surprised at the change. She who was formerly so careful, so dainty, now passed whole days without dressing, wore grey cotton stockings, and burnt tallow candles. She kept saying they must be economical since they were not rich, adding that she was very contented, very happy, that Tostes pleased her very much, with other speeches that closed the mouth of her mother-in-law. Besides, Emma no longer seemed inclined to follow her advice; once even, Madame Bovary having thought fit to maintain that mistresses ought to keep an eye on the religion of their servants, she had answered with so angry a look and so cold a smile that the good woman did not interfere again.

Emma was growing difficult, capricious. She ordered dishes for herself, then she did not touch them; one day drank only pure milk, the next cups of tea by the dozen. Often she persisted in not going out, then, stifling, threw open the windows and put on light dresses. After she had well scolded her servant she gave her presents or sent her out to see neighbours, just as she sometimes threw beggars all the silver in her purse, although she was by no means tender-hearted or easily accessible to the feelings of others, like most country-bred people, who always retain in their souls something of the horny hardness of the paternal hands.

Towards the end of February old Rouault, in memory of his cure, himself brought his son-in-law a superb turkey, and stayed three days at Tostes. Charles being with his patients, Emma kept him company. He smoked in the room, spat on the firedogs, talked farming, calves, cows, poultry, and municipal council, so that when he left she closed the door on him with a feeling of satisfaction that surprised even herself. Moreover she no longer concealed her contempt for anything or anybody, and at times she set herself to express singular opinions, finding fault with that which others approved, and approving things perverse and immoral, all of which made her husband open his eyes widely.

Would this misery last for ever? Would she never issue from it? Yet she was as good as all the women who were living happily. She had seen duchesses at Vaubyessard with clumsier waists and commoner ways, and she execrated the injustice of God. She leant her head against the walls to weep; she envied lives of stir; longed for masked balls, for violent pleasures, with all the wildness that she did not know, but that these must surely yield.

She grew pale and suffered from palpitations of the heart.

Charles prescribed valerian and camphor baths. Everything that was tried only seemed to irritate her the more.

On certain days she chatted with feverish rapidity, and this over-excitement was suddenly followed by a state of torpor, in which she remained without speaking, without moving. What then revived her was pouring a bottle of eau-de-cologne over her arms.

As she was constantly complaining about Tostes, Charles fancied that her illness was no doubt due to some local cause, and fixing on this idea, began to think seriously of setting up elsewhere.

From that moment she drank vinegar, contracted a sharp little cough, and completely lost her appetite.

It cost Charles much to give up Tostes after living there four years and "when he was beginning to get on there." Yet if it must be! He took her to Rouen to see his old master. It was a nervous complaint: change of air was needed.

After looking about him on this side and on that, Charles learnt that in the Neufchatel arrondissement there was a considerable market town called Yonville-l'Abbaye, whose doctor, a Polish refugee, had decamped a week before. Then he wrote to the chemist of the place to ask the number of the population, the distance from the nearest doctor, what his predecessor had made a year, and so forth; and the answer being satisfactory, he made up his mind to move towards the spring, if Emma's health did not improve.

One day when, in view of her departure, she was tidying a drawer, something pricked her finger. It was a wire of her wedding bouquet. The orange blossoms were yellow with dust and the silver bordered satin ribbons frayed at the edges. She threw it into the fire. It flared up more quickly than dry straw. Then it was, like a red bush in the cinders, slowly devoured. She watched it burn.

The little pasteboard berries burst, the wire twisted, the gold lace melted; and the shriveled paper corollas, fluttering like black butterflies at the back of the stove, at last flew up the chimney.

When they left Tostes at the month of March, Madame Bovary was pregnant.

PART 2

Chapter 1

Yonville-l'Abbaye (so called from an old Capuchin abbey of which not even the ruins remain) is a market-town twenty-four miles from Rouen, between the Abbeville and Beauvais roads, at the foot of a valley watered by the Rieule, a little river that runs into the Andelle after turning three water-mills near its mouth, where there are a few trout that the lads amuse themselves by fishing for on Sundays.

We leave the highroad at La Boissiere and keep straight on to the top of the Leux hill, whence the valley is seen. The river that runs through it makes of it, as it were, two regions with distinct physiognomies—all on the left is pasture land, all of the right arable. The meadow stretches under a bulge of low hills to join at the back with the pasture land of the Bray country, while on the eastern side, the plain, gently rising, broadens out, showing as far as eye can follow its blond cornfields. The water, flowing by the grass, divides with a white line the colour of the roads and of the plains, and the country is like a great unfolded mantle with a green velvet cape bordered with a fringe of silver.

Before us, on the verge of the horizon, lie the oaks of the forest of Argueil, with the steeps of the Saint-Jean hills scarred from top to bottom with red irregular lines; they are rain tracks, and these brick-tones standing out in narrow streaks against the grey colour of the mountain are due to the quantity of iron springs that flow beyond in the neighboring country.

Here we are on the confines of Normandy, Picardy, and the Ile-de-France, a bastard land whose language is without accent and its landscape is without character. It is there that they make the worst Neufchatel cheeses of all the arrondissement; and, on the other hand, farming is costly because so much manure is needed to enrich this friable soil full of sand and flints.

Up to 1835 there was no practicable road for getting to Yonville, but about this time a cross-road was made which joins that of Abbeville to that of Amiens, and is occasionally used by the Rouen wagoners on their way to Flanders. Yonville-l'Abbaye has remained stationary in spite of its "new outlet." Instead of improving the soil, they persist in keeping up the pasture lands, however depreciated they may be in value, and the lazy borough, growing away from the plain, has naturally spread riverwards. It is seem from afar sprawling along the banks like a cowherd taking a siesta by the water-side.

At the foot of the hill beyond the bridge begins a roadway, planted with young aspens, that leads in a straight line to the first houses in the place. These, fenced in by hedges, are in the middle of courtyards full of straggling buildings, wine-presses, cart-sheds and distilleries scattered under thick trees, with ladders, poles, or scythes hung on to the branches. The thatched roofs, like fur caps drawn over eyes, reach down over about a third of the low windows, whose coarse convex glasses have knots in the middle like the bottoms of bottles. Against the plaster wall diagonally crossed by black joists, a meagre pear-tree sometimes leans and the ground-floors have at their door a small swing-gate to keep out the chicks that come pilfering crumbs of bread steeped in cider on the threshold. But the courtyards grow narrower, the houses closer together, and the fences disappear; a bundle of ferns swings under a window from the end of a broomstick; there is a blacksmith's forge and then a wheelwright's, with two or three new carts outside that partly block the way. Then across an open space appears a white house beyond a grass mound ornamented by a Cupid, his finger on his lips; two brass vases are at each end of a flight of steps; scutcheons* blaze upon the door. It is the notary's house, and the finest in the place.

The Church is on the other side of the street, twenty paces farther down, at the entrance of the square. The little cemetery that surrounds it, closed in by a wall breast high, is so full of graves that the old stones, level with the ground, form a continuous pavement, on which the grass of itself has marked out regular green squares. The church was rebuilt during the last years of the reign of Charles X. The wooden roof is beginning to rot from the top, and here and there has black hollows in its blue colour. Over the door, where the organ should be, is a loft for the men, with a spiral staircase that reverberates under their wooden shoes.

The daylight coming through the plain glass windows falls obliquely upon the pews ranged along the walls, which are adorned here and there with a straw mat bearing beneath it the words in large letters, "Mr. So-and-so's pew." Farther on, at a spot where the building narrows, the confessional forms a pendant to a statuette of the Virgin, clothed in a satin robe, coifed with a tulle veil sprinkled with silver stars, and with red cheeks, like an idol of the Sandwich Islands; and, finally, a

---

* The panonceaux that have to be hung over the doors of notaries.

copy of the "Holy Family, presented by the Minister of the Interior," overlooking the high altar, between four candlesticks, closes in the perspective. The choir stalls, of deal wood, have been left unpainted.

The market, that is to say, a tiled roof supported by some twenty posts, occupies of itself about half the public square of Yonville. The town hall, constructed "from the designs of a Paris architect," is a sort of Greek temple that forms the corner next to the chemist's shop. On the ground-floor are three Ionic columns and on the first floor a semicircular gallery, while the dome that crowns it is occupied by a Gallic cock, resting one foot upon the "Charte" and holding in the other the scales of Justice.

But that which most attracts the eye is opposite the Lion d'Or inn, the chemist's shop of Monsieur Homais. In the evening especially its argand lamp is lit up and the red and green jars that embellish his shop-front throw far across the street their two streams of colour; then across them as if in Bengal lights is seen the shadow of the chemist leaning over his desk. His house from top to bottom is placarded with inscriptions written in large hand, round hand, printed hand: "Vichy, Seltzer, Barege waters, blood purifiers, Raspail patent medicine, Arabian racahout, Darcet lozenges, Regnault paste, trusses, baths, hygienic chocolate," etc. And the signboard, which takes up all the breadth of the shop, bears in gold letters, "Homais, Chemist." Then at the back of the shop, behind the great scales fixed to the counter, the word "Laboratory" appears on a scroll above a glass door, which about half-way up once more repeats "Homais" in gold letters on a black ground.

Beyond this there is nothing to see at Yonville. The street (the only one) a gunshot in length and flanked by a few shops on either side stops short at the turn of the highroad. If it is left on the right hand and the foot of the Saint-Jean hills followed the cemetery is soon reached.

At the time of the cholera, in order to enlarge this, a piece of wall was pulled down, and three acres of land by its side purchased; but all the new portion is almost tenantless; the tombs, as heretofore, continue to crowd together towards the gate. The keeper, who is at once gravedigger and church beadle (thus making a double profit out of the parish corpses), has taken advantage of the unused plot of ground to plant potatoes there. From year to year, however, his small field grows smaller, and when there is an epidemic, he does not know whether to rejoice at the deaths or regret the burials.

"You live on the dead, Lestiboudois!" the curie at last said to him one day. This grim remark made him reflect; it checked him for some time;

but to this day he carries on the cultivation of his little tubers, and even maintains stoutly that they grow naturally.

Since the events about to be narrated, nothing in fact has changed at Yonville. The tin tricolour flag still swings at the top of the church-steeple; the two chintz streamers still flutter in the wind from the linen-draper's; the chemist's fetuses, like lumps of white amadou, rot more and more in their turbid alcohol, and above the big door of the inn the old golden lion, faded by rain, still shows passers-by its poodle mane.

On the evening when the Bovarys were to arrive at Yonville, Widow Lefrancois, the landlady of this inn, was so very busy that she sweated great drops as she moved her saucepans. To-morrow was market-day. The meat had to be cut beforehand, the fowls drawn, the soup and coffee made. Moreover, she had the boarders' meal to see to, and that of the doctor, his wife, and their servant; the billiard-room was echoing with bursts of laughter; three millers in a small parlour were calling for brandy; the wood was blazing, the brazen pan was hissing, and on the long kitchen table, amid the quarters of raw mutton, rose piles of plates that rattled with the shaking of the block on which spinach was being chopped.

From the poultry-yard was heard the screaming of the fowls whom the servant was chasing in order to wring their necks.

A man slightly marked with small-pox, in green leather slippers, and wearing a velvet cap with a gold tassel, was warming his back at the chimney. His face expressed nothing but self-satisfaction, and he appeared to take life as calmly as the goldfinch suspended over his head in its wicker cage: this was the chemist.

"Artemise!" shouted the landlady, "chop some wood, fill the water bottles, bring some brandy, look sharp! If only I knew what dessert to offer the guests you are expecting! Good heavens! Those furniture-movers are beginning their racket in the billiard-room again; and their van has been left before the front door! The 'Hirondelle' might run into it when it draws up. Call Polyte and tell him to put it up. Only think, Monsieur Homais, that since morning they have had about fifteen games, and drunk eight jars of cider! Why, they'll tear my cloth for me," she went on, looking at them from a distance, her strainer in her hand.

"That wouldn't be much of a loss," replied Monsieur Homais. "You would buy another."

"Another billiard-table!" exclaimed the widow.

"Since that one is coming to pieces, Madame Lefrancois. I tell you again you are doing yourself harm, much harm! And besides, players

GUSTAVE FLAUBERT

now want narrow pockets and heavy cues. Hazards aren't played now; everything is changed! One must keep pace with the times! Just look at Tellier!"

The hostess reddened with vexation. The chemist went on—

"You may say what you like; his table is better than yours; and if one were to think, for example, of getting up a patriotic pool for Poland or the sufferers from the Lyons floods—"

"It isn't beggars like him that'll frighten us," interrupted the landlady, shrugging her fat shoulders. "Come, come, Monsieur Homais; as long as the 'Lion d'Or' exists people will come to it. We've feathered our nest; while one of these days you'll find the 'Cafe Francais' closed with a big placard on the shutters. Change my billiard-table!" she went on, speaking to herself, "the table that comes in so handy for folding the washing, and on which, in the hunting season, I have slept six visitors! But that dawdler, Hivert, doesn't come!"

"Are you waiting for him for your gentlemen's dinner?"

"Wait for him! And what about Monsieur Binet? As the clock strikes six you'll see him come in, for he hasn't his equal under the sun for punctuality. He must always have his seat in the small parlour. He'd rather die than dine anywhere else. And so squeamish as he is, and so particular about the cider! Not like Monsieur Leon; he sometimes comes at seven, or even half-past, and he doesn't so much as look at what he eats. Such a nice young man! Never speaks a rough word!"

"Well, you see, there's a great difference between an educated man and an old carabineer who is now a tax-collector."

Six o'clock struck. Binet came in.

He wore a blue frock-coat falling in a straight line round his thin body, and his leather cap, with its lappets knotted over the top of his head with string, showed under the turned-up peak a bald forehead, flattened by the constant wearing of a helmet. He wore a black cloth waistcoat, a hair collar, grey trousers, and, all the year round, well-blacked boots, that had two parallel swellings due to the sticking out of his big-toes. Not a hair stood out from the regular line of fair whiskers, which, encircling his jaws, framed, after the fashion of a garden border, his long, wan face, whose eyes were small and the nose hooked. Clever at all games of cards, a good hunter, and writing a fine hand, he had at home a lathe, and amused himself by turning napkin rings, with which he filled up his house, with the jealousy of an artist and the egotism of a bourgeois.

He went to the small parlour, but the three millers had to be got out first, and during the whole time necessary for laying the cloth, Binet remained silent in his place near the stove. Then he shut the door and took off his cap in his usual way.

"It isn't with saying civil things that he'll wear out his tongue," said the chemist, as soon as he was along with the landlady.

"He never talks more," she replied. "Last week two travelers in the cloth line were here—such clever chaps who told such jokes in the evening, that I fairly cried with laughing; and he stood there like a dab fish and never said a word."

"Yes," observed the chemist; "no imagination, no sallies, nothing that makes the society-man."

"Yet they say he has parts," objected the landlady.

"Parts!" replied Monsieur Homais; "he, parts! In his own line it is possible," he added in a calmer tone. And he went on—

"Ah! That a merchant, who has large connections, a jurisconsult, a doctor, a chemist, should be thus absent-minded, that they should become whimsical or even peevish, I can understand; such cases are cited in history. But at least it is because they are thinking of something. Myself, for example, how often has it happened to me to look on the bureau for my pen to write a label, and to find, after all, that I had put it behind my ear!"

Madame Lefrancois just then went to the door to see if the "Hirondelle" were not coming. She started. A man dressed in black suddenly came into the kitchen. By the last gleam of the twilight one could see that his face was rubicund and his form athletic.

"What can I do for you, Monsieur le Curie?" asked the landlady, as she reached down from the chimney one of the copper candlesticks placed with their candles in a row. "Will you take something? A thimbleful of Cassis*? A glass of wine?"

The priest declined very politely. He had come for his umbrella, that he had forgotten the other day at the Ernemont convent, and after asking Madame Lefrancois to have it sent to him at the presbytery in the evening, he left for the church, from which the Angelus was ringing.

When the chemist no longer heard the noise of his boots along the square, he thought the priest's behaviour just now very unbecoming. This refusal to take any refreshment seemed to him the most odious

---

* Black currant liqueur.

GUSTAVE FLAUBERT

hypocrisy; all priests tippled on the sly, and were trying to bring back the days of the tithe.

The landlady took up the defence of her curie.

"Besides, he could double up four men like you over his knee. Last year he helped our people to bring in the straw; he carried as many as six trusses at once, he is so strong."

"Bravo!" said the chemist. "Now just send your daughters to confess to fellows which such a temperament! I, if I were the Government, I'd have the priests bled once a month. Yes, Madame Lefrancois, every month—a good phlebotomy, in the interests of the police and morals."

"Be quiet, Monsieur Homais. You are an infidel; you've no religion."

The chemist answered: "I have a religion, my religion, and I even have more than all these others with their mummeries and their juggling. I adore God, on the contrary. I believe in the Supreme Being, in a Creator, whatever he may be. I care little who has placed us here below to fulfil our duties as citizens and fathers of families; but I don't need to go to church to kiss silver plates, and fatten, out of my pocket, a lot of good-for-nothings who live better than we do. For one can know Him as well in a wood, in a field, or even contemplating the eternal vault like the ancients. My God! Mine is the God of Socrates, of Franklin, of Voltaire, and of Beranger! I am for the profession of faith of the 'Savoyard Vicar,' and the immortal principles of '89! And I can't admit of an old boy of a God who takes walks in his garden with a cane in his hand, who lodges his friends in the belly of whales, dies uttering a cry, and rises again at the end of three days; things absurd in themselves, and completely opposed, moreover, to all physical laws, which prove to us, by the way, that priests have always wallowed in turpid ignorance, in which they would fain engulf the people with them."

He ceased, looking round for an audience, for in his bubbling over the chemist had for a moment fancied himself in the midst of the town council. But the landlady no longer heeded him; she was listening to a distant rolling. One could distinguish the noise of a carriage mingled with the clattering of loose horseshoes that beat against the ground, and at last the "Hirondelle" stopped at the door.

It was a yellow box on two large wheels, that, reaching to the tilt, prevented travelers from seeing the road and dirtied their shoulders. The small panes of the narrow windows rattled in their sashes when the coach was closed, and retained here and there patches of mud amid the old layers of dust, that not even storms of rain had altogether washed away. It was drawn by three horses, the first a leader, and when it came down-hill its bottom jolted against the ground.

Some of the inhabitants of Yonville came out into the square; they all spoke at once, asking for news, for explanations, for hampers. Hivert did not know whom to answer. It was he who did the errands of the place in town. He went to the shops and brought back rolls of leather for the shoemaker, old iron for the farrier, a barrel of herrings for his mistress, caps from the milliner's, locks from the hair-dresser's and all along the road on his return journey he distributed his parcels, which he threw, standing upright on his seat and shouting at the top of his voice, over the enclosures of the yards.

An accident had delayed him. Madame Bovary's greyhound had run across the field. They had whistled for him a quarter of an hour; Hivert had even gone back a mile and a half expecting every moment to catch sight of her; but it had been necessary to go on.

Emma had wept, grown angry; she had accused Charles of this misfortune. Monsieur Lheureux, a draper, who happened to be in the coach with her, had tried to console her by a number of examples of lost dogs recognizing their masters at the end of long years. One, he said had been told of, who had come back to Paris from Constantinople. Another had gone one hundred and fifty miles in a straight line, and swum four rivers; and his own father had possessed a poodle, which, after twelve years of absence, had all of a sudden jumped on his back in the street as he was going to dine in town.

Chapter 2

E mma got out first, then Felicite, Monsieur Lheureux, and a nurse, and they had to wake up Charles in his corner, where he had slept soundly since night set in.

Homais introduced himself; he offered his homages to madame and his respects to monsieur; said he was charmed to have been able to render them some slight service, and added with a cordial air that he had ventured to invite himself, his wife being away.

When Madame Bovary was in the kitchen she went up to the chimney.

With the tips of her fingers she caught her dress at the knee, and having thus pulled it up to her ankle, held out her foot in its black boot to the fire above the revolving leg of mutton. The flame lit up the whole of her, penetrating with a crude light the woof of her gowns, the fine pores of her fair skin, and even her eyelids, which she blinked now and again. A great red glow passed over her with the blowing of the wind through the half-open door.

On the other side of the chimney a young man with fair hair watched her silently.

As he was a good deal bored at Yonville, where he was a clerk at the notary's, Monsieur Guillaumin, Monsieur Leon Dupuis (it was he who was the second habitue of the "Lion d'Or") frequently put back his dinner-hour in hope that some traveler might come to the inn, with whom he could chat in the evening. On the days when his work was done early, he had, for want of something else to do, to come punctually, and endure from soup to cheese a tete-a-tete with Binet. It was therefore with delight that he accepted the landlady's suggestion that he should dine in company with the newcomers, and they passed into the large parlour where Madame Lefrancois, for the purpose of showing off, had had the table laid for four.

Homais asked to be allowed to keep on his skull-cap, for fear of coryza; then, turning to his neighbour—

"Madame is no doubt a little fatigued; one gets jolted so abominably in our 'Hirondelle.'"

"That is true," replied Emma; "but moving about always amuses me. I like change of place."

"It is so tedious," sighed the clerk, "to be always riveted to the same places."

"If you were like me," said Charles, "constantly obliged to be in the saddle"—

"But," Leon went on, addressing himself to Madame Bovary, "nothing, it seems to me, is more pleasant—when one can," he added.

"Moreover," said the druggist, "the practice of medicine is not very hard work in our part of the world, for the state of our roads allows us the use of gigs, and generally, as the farmers are prosperous, they pay pretty well. We have, medically speaking, besides the ordinary cases of enteritis, bronchitis, bilious affections, etc., now and then a few intermittent fevers at harvest-time; but on the whole, little of a serious nature, nothing special to note, unless it be a great deal of scrofula, due, no doubt, to the deplorable hygienic conditions of our peasant dwellings. Ah! you will find many prejudices to combat, Monsieur Bovary, much obstinacy of routine, with which all the efforts of your science will daily come into collision; for people still have recourse to novenas, to relics, to the priest, rather than come straight to the doctor or the chemist. The climate, however, is not, truth to tell, bad, and we even have a few nonagenarians in our parish. The thermometer (I have made some observations) falls in winter to 4 degrees Centigrade at the outside, which gives us 24 degrees Reaumur as the maximum, or otherwise 54 degrees Fahrenheit (English scale), not more. And, as a matter of fact, we are sheltered from the north winds by the forest of Argueil on the one side, from the west winds by the St. Jean range on the other; and this heat, moreover, which, on account of the aqueous vapours given off by the river and the considerable number of cattle in the fields, which, as you know, exhale much ammonia, that is to say, nitrogen, hydrogen and oxygen (no, nitrogen and hydrogen alone), and which sucking up into itself the humus from the ground, mixing together all those different emanations, unites them into a stack, so to say, and combining with the electricity diffused through the atmosphere, when there is any, might in the long run, as in tropical countries, engender insalubrious miasmata—this heat, I say, finds itself perfectly tempered on the side whence it comes, or rather whence it should come—that is to say, the southern side—by the south-eastern winds, which, having cooled themselves passing over the Seine, reach us sometimes all at once like breezes from Russia."

"At any rate, you have some walks in the neighbourhood?" continued Madame Bovary, speaking to the young man.

"Oh, very few," he answered. "There is a place they call La Pature, on the top of the hill, on the edge of the forest. Sometimes, on Sundays, I go and stay there with a book, watching the sunset."

"I think there is nothing so admirable as sunsets," she resumed; "but especially by the side of the sea."

"Oh, I adore the sea!" said Monsieur Leon.

"And then, does it not seem to you," continued Madame Bovary, "that the mind travels more freely on this limitless expanse, the contemplation of which elevates the soul, gives ideas of the infinite, the ideal?"

"It is the same with mountainous landscapes," continued Leon. "A cousin of mine who travelled in Switzerland last year told me that one could not picture to oneself the poetry of the lakes, the charm of the waterfalls, the gigantic effect of the glaciers. One sees pines of incredible size across torrents, cottages suspended over precipices, and, a thousand feet below one, whole valleys when the clouds open. Such spectacles must stir to enthusiasm, incline to prayer, to ecstasy; and I no longer marvel at that celebrated musician who, the better to inspire his imagination, was in the habit of playing the piano before some imposing site."

"You play?" she asked.

"No, but I am very fond of music," he replied.

"Ah! don't you listen to him, Madame Bovary," interrupted Homais, bending over his plate. "That's sheer modesty. Why, my dear fellow, the other day in your room you were singing 'L'Ange Gardien' ravishingly. I heard you from the laboratory. You gave it like an actor."

Leon, in fact, lodged at the chemist's where he had a small room on the second floor, overlooking the Place. He blushed at the compliment of his landlord, who had already turned to the doctor, and was enumerating to him, one after the other, all the principal inhabitants of Yonville. He was telling anecdotes, giving information; the fortune of the notary was not known exactly, and "there was the Tuvache household," who made a good deal of show.

Emma continued, "And what music do you prefer?"

"Oh, German music; that which makes you dream."

"Have you been to the opera?"

"Not yet; but I shall go next year, when I am living at Paris to finish reading for the bar."

"As I had the honour of putting it to your husband," said the chemist, "with regard to this poor Yanoda who has run away, you will find yourself, thanks to his extravagance, in the possession of one of the most comfortable houses of Yonville. Its greatest convenience for a doctor is a door giving on the Walk, where one can go in and out unseen. Moreover, it contains everything that is agreeable in a household—a laundry, kitchen with offices, sitting-room, fruit-room, and so on. He was a gay dog, who didn't care what he spent. At the end of the garden, by the side of the water, he had an arbour built just for the purpose of drinking beer in summer; and if madame is fond of gardening she will be able—"

"My wife doesn't care about it," said Charles; "although she has been advised to take exercise, she prefers always sitting in her room reading."

"Like me," replied Leon. "And indeed, what is better than to sit by one's fireside in the evening with a book, while the wind beats against the window and the lamp is burning?"

"What, indeed?" she said, fixing her large black eyes wide open upon him.

"One thinks of nothing," he continued; "the hours slip by. Motionless we traverse countries we fancy we see, and your thought, blending with the fiction, playing with the details, follows the outline of the adventures. It mingles with the characters, and it seems as if it were yourself palpitating beneath their costumes."

"That is true! That is true?" she said.

"Has it ever happened to you," Leon went on, "to come across some vague idea of one's own in a book, some dim image that comes back to you from afar, and as the completest expression of your own slightest sentiment?"

"I have experienced it," she replied.

"That is why," he said, "I especially love the poets. I think verse more tender than prose, and that it moves far more easily to tears."

"Still in the long run it is tiring," continued Emma. "Now I, on the contrary, adore stories that rush breathlessly along, that frighten one. I detest commonplace heroes and moderate sentiments, such as there are in nature."

"In fact," observed the clerk, "these works, not touching the heart, miss, it seems to me, the true end of art. It is so sweet, amid all the disenchantments of life, to be able to dwell in thought upon noble characters, pure affections, and pictures of happiness. For myself, living here far from the world, this is my one distraction; but Yonville affords so few resources."

"Like Tostes, no doubt," replied Emma; "and so I always subscribed to a lending library."

"If madame will do me the honour of making use of it", said the chemist, who had just caught the last words, "I have at her disposal a library composed of the best authors, Voltaire, Rousseau, Delille, Walter Scott, the 'Echo des Feuilletons'; and in addition I receive various periodicals, among them the 'Fanal de Rouen' daily, having the advantage to be its correspondent for the districts of Buchy, Forges, Neufchatel, Yonville, and vicinity."

For two hours and a half they had been at table; for the servant Artemis, carelessly dragging her old list slippers over the flags, brought one plate after the other, forgot everything, and constantly left the door of the billiard-room half open, so that it beat against the wall with its hooks.

Unconsciously, Leon, while talking, had placed his foot on one of the bars of the chair on which Madame Bovary was sitting. She wore a small blue silk necktie, that kept up like a ruff a gauffered cambric collar, and with the movements of her head the lower part of her face gently sunk into the linen or came out from it. Thus side by side, while Charles and the chemist chatted, they entered into one of those vague conversations where the hazard of all that is said brings you back to the fixed centre of a common sympathy. The Paris theatres, titles of novels, new quadrilles, and the world they did not know; Tostes, where she had lived, and Yonville, where they were; they examined all, talked of everything till to the end of dinner.

When coffee was served Felicite went away to get ready the room in the new house, and the guests soon raised the siege. Madame Lefrancois was asleep near the cinders, while the stable-boy, lantern in hand, was waiting to show Monsieur and Madame Bovary the way home. Bits of straw stuck in his red hair, and he limped with his left leg. When he had taken in his other hand the cure's umbrella, they started.

The town was asleep; the pillars of the market threw great shadows; the earth was all grey as on a summer's night. But as the doctor's house was only some fifty paces from the inn, they had to say good-night almost immediately, and the company dispersed.

As soon as she entered the passage, Emma felt the cold of the plaster fall about her shoulders like damp linen. The walls were new and the wooden stairs creaked. In their bedroom, on the first floor, a whitish light passed through the curtainless windows.

She could catch glimpses of tree tops, and beyond, the fields, half-drowned in the fog that lay reeking in the moonlight along the course of the river. In the middle of the room, pell-mell, were scattered drawers, bottles, curtain-rods, gilt poles, with mattresses on the chairs and basins on the ground—the two men who had brought the furniture had left everything about carelessly.

This was the fourth time that she had slept in a strange place.

The first was the day of her going to the convent; the second, of her arrival at Tostes; the third, at Vaubyessard; and this was the fourth. And each one had marked, as it were, the inauguration of a new phase in her life. She did not believe that things could present themselves in the same way in different places, and since the portion of her life lived had been bad, no doubt that which remained to be lived would be better.

Chapter 3

The next day, as she was getting up, she saw the clerk on the Place. She had on a dressing-gown. He looked up and bowed. She nodded quickly and reclosed the window.

Leon waited all day for six o'clock in the evening to come, but on going to the inn, he found no one but Monsieur Binet, already at table. The dinner of the evening before had been a considerable event for him; he had never till then talked for two hours consecutively to a "lady." How then had he been able to explain, and in such language, the number of things that he could not have said so well before? He was usually shy, and maintained that reserve which partakes at once of modesty and dissimulation.

At Yonville he was considered "well-bred." He listened to the arguments of the older people, and did not seem hot about politics—a remarkable thing for a young man. Then he had some accomplishments; he painted in water-colours, could read the key of G, and readily talked literature after dinner when he did not play cards. Monsieur Homais respected him for his education; Madame Homais liked him for his good-nature, for he often took the little Homais into the garden—little brats who were always dirty, very much spoilt, and somewhat lymphatic, like their mother. Besides the servant to look after them, they had Justin, the chemist's apprentice, a second cousin of Monsieur Homais, who had been taken into the house from charity, and who was useful at the same time as a servant.

The druggist proved the best of neighbours. He gave Madame Bovary information as to the trades-people, sent expressly for his own cider merchant, tasted the drink himself, and saw that the casks were properly placed in the cellar; he explained how to set about getting in a supply of butter cheap, and made an arrangement with Lestiboudois, the sacristan, who, besides his sacerdotal and funeral functions, looked after the principal gardens at Yonville by the hour or the year, according to the taste of the customers.

The need of looking after others was not the only thing that urged the chemist to such obsequious cordiality; there was a plan underneath it all.

He had infringed the law of the 19th Ventose, year xi., article I, which forbade all persons not having a diploma to practise medicine;

so that, after certain anonymous denunciations, Homais had been summoned to Rouen to see the procurer of the king in his own private room; the magistrate receiving him standing up, ermine on shoulder and cap on head. It was in the morning, before the court opened. In the corridors one heard the heavy boots of the gendarmes walking past, and like a far-off noise great locks that were shut. The druggist's ears tingled as if he were about to have an apoplectic stroke; he saw the depths of dungeons, his family in tears, his shop sold, all the jars dispersed; and he was obliged to enter a cafe and take a glass of rum and seltzer to recover his spirits.

Little by little the memory of this reprimand grew fainter, and he continued, as heretofore, to give anodyne consultations in his back-parlour. But the mayor resented it, his colleagues were jealous, everything was to be feared; gaining over Monsieur Bovary by his attentions was to earn his gratitude, and prevent his speaking out later on, should he notice anything. So every morning Homais brought him "the paper," and often in the afternoon left his shop for a few moments to have a chat with the Doctor.

Charles was dull: patients did not come. He remained seated for hours without speaking, went into his consulting room to sleep, or watched his wife sewing. Then for diversion he employed himself at home as a workman; he even tried to do up the attic with some paint which had been left behind by the painters. But money matters worried him. He had spent so much for repairs at Tostes, for madame's toilette, and for the moving, that the whole dowry, over three thousand crowns, had slipped away in two years.

Then how many things had been spoilt or lost during their carriage from Tostes to Yonville, without counting the plaster cure, who falling out of the coach at an over-severe jolt, had been dashed into a thousand fragments on the pavements of Quincampoix! A pleasanter trouble came to distract him, namely, the pregnancy of his wife. As the time of her confinement approached he cherished her the more. It was another bond of the flesh establishing itself, and, as it were, a continued sentiment of a more complex union. When from afar he saw her languid walk, and her figure without stays turning softly on her hips; when opposite one another he looked at her at his ease, while she took tired poses in her armchair, then his happiness knew no bounds; he got up, embraced her, passed his hands over her face, called her little mamma, wanted to make her dance, and half-laughing, half-crying, uttered all kinds of caressing pleasantries that came into his head. The idea of having begotten a child delighted him. Now he wanted nothing. He knew human life from end to end, and he sat down to it with serenity.

Emma at first felt a great astonishment; then was anxious to be delivered that she might know what it was to be a mother. But not being able to spend as much as she would have liked, to have a swing-bassinette with rose silk curtains, and embroidered caps, in a fit of bitterness she gave up looking after the trousseau, and ordered the whole of it from a village needlewoman, without choosing or discussing anything. Thus she did not amuse herself with those preparations that stimulate the tenderness of mothers, and so her affection was from the very outset, perhaps, to some extent attenuated.

As Charles, however, spoke of the boy at every meal, she soon began to think of him more consecutively.

She hoped for a son; he would be strong and dark; she would call him George; and this idea of having a male child was like an expected revenge for all her impotence in the past. A man, at least, is free; he may travel over passions and over countries, overcome obstacles, taste of the most far-away pleasures. But a woman is always hampered. At once inert and flexible, she has against her the weakness of the flesh and legal dependence. Her will, like the veil of her bonnet, held by a string, flutters in every wind; there is always some desire that draws her, some conventionality that restrains.

She was confined on a Sunday at about six o'clock, as the sun was rising.

"It is a girl!" said Charles.

She turned her head away and fainted.

Madame Homais, as well as Madame Lefrancois of the Lion d'Or, almost immediately came running in to embrace her. The chemist, as man of discretion, only offered a few provincial felicitations through the half-opened door. He wished to see the child and thought it well made.

Whilst she was getting well she occupied herself much in seeking a name for her daughter. First she went over all those that have Italian endings, such as Clara, Louisa, Amanda, Atala; she liked Galsuinde pretty well, and Yseult or Leocadie still better.

Charles wanted the child to be called after her mother; Emma opposed this. They ran over the calendar from end to end, and then consulted outsiders.

"Monsieur Leon," said the chemist, "with whom I was talking about it the other day, wonders you do not chose Madeleine. It is very much in fashion just now."

But Madame Bovary, senior, cried out loudly against this name of a sinner. As to Monsieur Homais, he had a preference for all those that recalled some great man, an illustrious fact, or a generous idea, and it was on this system that he had baptized his four children. Thus Napoleon represented glory and Franklin liberty; Irma was perhaps a concession to romanticism, but Athalie was a homage to the greatest masterpiece of the French stage. For his philosophical convictions did not interfere with his artistic tastes; in him the thinker did not stifle the man of sentiment; he could make distinctions, make allowances for imagination and fanaticism. In this tragedy, for example, he found fault with the ideas, but admired the style; he detested the conception, but applauded all the details, and loathed the characters while he grew enthusiastic over their dialogue. When he read the fine passages he was transported, but when he thought that mummers would get something out of them for their show, he was disconsolate; and in this confusion of sentiments in which he was involved he would have liked at once to crown Racine with both his hands and discuss with him for a good quarter of an hour.

At last Emma remembered that at the chateau of Vaubyessard she had heard the Marchioness call a young lady Berthe; from that moment this name was chosen; and as old Rouault could not come, Monsieur Homais was requested to stand godfather. His gifts were all products from his establishment, to wit: six boxes of jujubes, a whole jar of racahout, three cakes of marshmallow paste, and six sticks of sugar-candy into the bargain that he had come across in a cupboard. On the evening of the ceremony there was a grand dinner; the cure was present; there was much excitement. Monsieur Homais towards liqueur-time began singing "Le Dieu des bonnes gens." Monsieur Leon sang a barcarolle, and Madame Bovary, senior, who was godmother, a romance of the time of the Empire; finally, M. Bovary, senior, insisted on having the child brought down, and began baptizing it with a glass of champagne that he poured over its head. This mockery of the first of the sacraments made the Abbe Bournisien angry; old Bovary replied by a quotation from "La Guerre des Dieux"; the cure wanted to leave; the ladies implored, Homais interfered; and they succeeded in making the priest sit down again, and he quietly went on with the half-finished coffee in his saucer.

Monsieur Bovary, senior, stayed at Yonville a month, dazzling the natives by a superb policeman's cap with silver tassels that he wore in the morning when he smoked his pipe in the square. Being also in the habit of drinking a good deal of brandy, he often sent the servant to the Lion d'Or to buy him a bottle, which was put down to his son's account, and to perfume his handkerchiefs he used up his daughter-in-law's whole supply of eau-de-cologne.

The latter did not at all dislike his company. He had knocked about the world, he talked about Berlin, Vienna, and Strasbourg, of his soldier times, of the mistresses he had had, the grand luncheons of which he had partaken; then he was amiable, and sometimes even, either on the stairs, or in the garden, would seize hold of her waist, crying, "Charles, look out for yourself."

Then Madame Bovary, senior, became alarmed for her son's happiness, and fearing that her husband might in the long-run have an immoral influence upon the ideas of the young woman, took care to hurry their departure. Perhaps she had more serious reasons for uneasiness. Monsieur Bovary was not the man to respect anything.

One day Emma was suddenly seized with the desire to see her little girl, who had been put to nurse with the carpenter's wife, and, without looking at the calendar to see whether the six weeks of the Virgin were yet passed, she set out for the Rollets' house, situated at the extreme end of the village, between the highroad and the fields.

It was mid-day, the shutters of the houses were closed and the slate roofs that glittered beneath the fierce light of the blue sky seemed to strike sparks from the crest of the gables. A heavy wind was blowing; Emma felt weak as she walked; the stones of the pavement hurt her; she was doubtful whether she would not go home again, or go in somewhere to rest.

At this moment Monsieur Leon came out from a neighbouring door with a bundle of papers under his arm. He came to greet her, and stood in the shade in front of the Lheureux's shop under the projecting grey awning.

Madame Bovary said she was going to see her baby, but that she was beginning to grow tired.

"If—" said Leon, not daring to go on.

"Have you any business to attend to?" she asked.

And on the clerk's answer, she begged him to accompany her. That same evening this was known in Yonville, and Madame Tuvache, the mayor's wife, declared in the presence of her servant that "Madame Bovary was compromising herself."

To get to the nurse's it was necessary to turn to the left on leaving the street, as if making for the cemetery, and to follow between little houses and yards a small path bordered with privet hedges. They were in bloom, and so were the speedwells, eglantines, thistles, and the sweetbriar that sprang up from the thickets. Through openings in the hedges one could see into the huts, some pigs on a dung-heap, or tethered cows rubbing their horns against the trunk of trees. The two, side by side walked slowly, she leaning upon him, and he restraining his pace, which he regulated by hers; in front of them a swarm of midges fluttered, buzzing in the warm air.

They recognized the house by an old walnut-tree which shaded it.

Low and covered with brown tiles, there hung outside it, beneath the dormer-window of the garret, a string of onions. Faggots upright against a thorn fence surrounded a bed of lettuce, a few square feet of lavender, and sweet peas strung on sticks. Dirty water was running here and there on the grass, and all round were several indefinite rags, knitted stockings, a red calico jacket, and a large sheet of coarse linen spread over the hedge. At the noise of the gate the nurse appeared with a baby she was suckling on one arm. With her other hand she was pulling along a poor puny little fellow, his face covered with scrofula, the son of a Rouen hosier, whom his parents, too taken up with their business, left in the country.

"Go in," she said; "your little one is there asleep."

The room on the ground-floor, the only one in the dwelling, had at its farther end, against the wall, a large bed without curtains, while a kneading-trough took up the side by the window, one pane of which was mended with a piece of blue paper. In the corner behind the door, shining hob-nailed shoes stood in a row under the slab of the washstand, near a bottle of oil with a feather stuck in its mouth; a Matthieu Laensberg lay on the dusty mantelpiece amid gunflints, candle-ends, and bits of amadou.

Finally, the last luxury in the apartment was a "Fame" blowing her trumpets, a picture cut out, no doubt, from some perfumer's prospectus and nailed to the wall with six wooden shoe-pegs.

Emma's child was asleep in a wicker-cradle. She took it up in the wrapping that enveloped it and began singing softly as she rocked herself to and fro.

Leon walked up and down the room; it seemed strange to him to see this beautiful woman in her nankeen dress in the midst of all this poverty. Madam Bovary reddened; he turned away, thinking perhaps there had been an impertinent look in his eyes. Then she put back the little girl, who had just been sick over her collar.

The nurse at once came to dry her, protesting that it wouldn't show.

"She gives me other doses," she said: "I am always a-washing of her. If you would have the goodness to order Camus, the grocer, to let me have a little soap, it would really be more convenient for you, as I needn't trouble you then."

"Very well! very well!" said Emma. "Good morning, Madame Rollet," and she went out, wiping her shoes at the door.

The good woman accompanied her to the end of the garden, talking all the time of the trouble she had getting up of nights.

"I'm that worn out sometimes as I drop asleep on my chair. I'm sure you might at least give me just a pound of ground coffee; that'd last me a month, and I'd take it of a morning with some milk."

After having submitted to her thanks, Madam Bovary left. She had gone a little way down the path when, at the sound of wooden shoes, she turned round. It was the nurse.

"What is it?"

Then the peasant woman, taking her aside behind an elm tree, began talking to her of her husband, who with his trade and six francs a year that the captain—

"Oh, be quick!" said Emma.

"Well," the nurse went on, heaving sighs between each word, "I'm afraid he'll be put out seeing me have coffee alone, you know men—"

"But you are to have some," Emma repeated; "I will give you some. You bother me!"

"Oh, dear! my poor, dear lady! you see in consequence of his wounds he has terrible cramps in the chest. He even says that cider weakens him."

"Do make haste, Mere Rollet!"

"Well," the latter continued, making a curtsey, "if it weren't asking too much," and she curtsied once more, "if you would"—and her eyes begged—"a jar of brandy," she said at last, "and I'd rub your little one's feet with it; they're as tender as one's tongue."

Once rid of the nurse, Emma again took Monsieur Leon's arm. She walked fast for some time, then more slowly, and looking straight in front of her, her eyes rested on the shoulder of the young man, whose frock-coat had a black-velvety collar. His brown hair fell over it, straight and carefully arranged. She noticed his nails which were longer than one wore them at Yonville. It was one of the clerk's chief occupations to trim them, and for this purpose he kept a special knife in his writing desk.

They returned to Yonville by the water-side. In the warm season the bank, wider than at other times, showed to their foot the garden walls whence a few steps led to the river. It flowed noiselessly, swift, and cold to the eye; long, thin grasses huddled together in it as the current drove them, and spread themselves upon the limpid water like streaming hair; sometimes at the tip of the reeds or on the leaf of a water-lily an insect with fine legs crawled or rested. The sun pierced with a ray the small blue bubbles of the waves that, breaking, followed each other; branchless old willows mirrored their grey backs in the water; beyond, all around, the meadows seemed empty. It was the dinner-hour at the farms, and the young woman and her companion heard nothing as they walked but the fall of their steps on the earth of the path, the words they spoke, and the sound of Emma's dress rustling round her.

The walls of the gardens with pieces of bottle on their coping were hot as the glass windows of a conservatory. Wallflowers had sprung up between the bricks, and with the tip of her open sunshade Madame Bovary, as she passed, made some of their faded flowers crumble into a yellow dust, or a spray of overhanging honeysuckle and clematis caught in its fringe and dangled for a moment over the silk.

They were talking of a troupe of Spanish dancers who were expected shortly at the Rouen theatre.

"Are you going?" she asked.

"If I can," he answered.

Had they nothing else to say to one another? Yet their eyes were full of more serious speech, and while they forced themselves to find trivial phrases, they felt the same languor stealing over them both. It was the whisper of the soul, deep, continuous, dominating that of their voices. Surprised with wonder at this strange sweetness, they did not think of speaking of the sensation or of seeking its cause. Coming joys, like tropical shores, throw over the immensity before them their inborn softness, an odorous wind, and we are lulled by this intoxication without a thought of the horizon that we do not even know.

In one place the ground had been trodden down by the cattle; they had to step on large green stones put here and there in the mud.

She often stopped a moment to look where to place her foot, and tottering on a stone that shook, her arms outspread, her form bent forward with a look of indecision, she would laugh, afraid of falling into the puddles of water.

When they arrived in front of her garden, Madame Bovary opened the little gate, ran up the steps and disappeared.

Leon returned to his office. His chief was away; he just glanced at the briefs, then cut himself a pen, and at last took up his hat and went out.

He went to La Pature at the top of the Argueil hills at the beginning of the forest; he threw himself upon the ground under the pines and watched the sky through his fingers.

"How bored I am!" he said to himself, "how bored I am!"

He thought he was to be pitied for living in this village, with Homais for a friend and Monsieru Guillaumin for master. The latter, entirely absorbed by his business, wearing gold-rimmed spectacles and red whiskers over a white cravat, understood nothing of mental refinements, although he affected a stiff English manner, which in the beginning had impressed the clerk.

As to the chemist's spouse, she was the best wife in Normandy, gentle as a sheep, loving her children, her father, her mother, her cousins, weeping for other's woes, letting everything go in her household, and detesting corsets; but so slow of movement, such a bore to listen to, so common in appearance, and of such restricted conversation, that although she was thirty, he only twenty, although they slept in rooms next each other and he spoke to her daily, he never thought that she might be a woman for another, or that she possessed anything else of her sex than the gown.

And what else was there? Binet, a few shopkeepers, two or three publicans, the cure, and finally, Monsieur Tuvache, the mayor, with his two sons, rich, crabbed, obtuse persons, who farmed their own lands and had feasts among themselves, bigoted to boot, and quite unbearable companions.

But from the general background of all these human faces Emma's stood out isolated and yet farthest off; for between her and him he seemed to see a vague abyss.

In the beginning he had called on her several times along with the druggist. Charles had not appeared particularly anxious to see him again, and Leon did not know what to do between his fear of being indiscreet and the desire for an intimacy that seemed almost impossible.

Chapter 4

When the first cold days set in Emma left her bedroom for the sitting-room, a long apartment with a low ceiling, in which there was on the mantelpiece a large bunch of coral spread out against the looking-glass. Seated in her arm chair near the window, she could see the villagers pass along the pavement.

Twice a day Leon went from his office to the Lion d'Or. Emma could hear him coming from afar; she leant forward listening, and the young man glided past the curtain, always dressed in the same way, and without turning his head. But in the twilight, when, her chin resting on her left hand, she let the embroidery she had begun fall on her knees, she often shuddered at the apparition of this shadow suddenly gliding past. She would get up and order the table to be laid.

Monsieur Homais called at dinner-time. Skull-cap in hand, he came in on tiptoe, in order to disturb no one, always repeating the same phrase, "Good evening, everybody." Then, when he had taken his seat at the table between the pair, he asked the doctor about his patients, and the latter consulted his as to the probability of their payment. Next they talked of "what was in the paper."

Homais by this hour knew it almost by heart, and he repeated it from end to end, with the reflections of the penny-a-liners, and all the stories of individual catastrophes that had occurred in France or abroad. But the subject becoming exhausted, he was not slow in throwing out some remarks on the dishes before him.

Sometimes even, half-rising, he delicately pointed out to madame the tenderest morsel, or turning to the servant, gave her some advice on the manipulation of stews and the hygiene of seasoning.

He talked aroma, osmazome, juices, and gelatine in a bewildering manner. Moreover, Homais, with his head fuller of recipes than his shop of jars, excelled in making all kinds of preserves, vinegars, and sweet liqueurs; he knew also all the latest inventions in economic stoves, together with the art of preserving cheese and of curing sick wines.

At eight o'clock Justin came to fetch him to shut up the shop.

Then Monsieur Homais gave him a sly look, especially if Felicite was there, for he half noticed that his apprentice was fond of the doctor's house.

"The young dog," he said, "is beginning to have ideas, and the devil take me if I don't believe he's in love with your servant!"

But a more serious fault with which he reproached Justin was his constantly listening to conversation. On Sunday, for example, one could not get him out of the drawing-room, whither Madame Homais had called him to fetch the children, who were falling asleep in the armchairs, and dragging down with their backs calico chair-covers that were too large.

Not many people came to these soirees at the chemist's, his scandal-mongering and political opinions having successfully alienated various respectable persons from him. The clerk never failed to be there. As soon as he heard the bell he ran to meet Madame Bovary, took her shawl, and put away under the shop-counter the thick list shoes that she wore over her boots when there was snow.

First they played some hands at trente-et-un; next Monsieur Homais played ecarte with Emma; Leon behind her gave her advice.

Standing up with his hands on the back of her chair he saw the teeth of her comb that bit into her chignon. With every movement that she made to throw her cards the right side of her dress was drawn up. From her turned-up hair a dark colour fell over her back, and growing gradually paler, lost itself little by little in the shade. Then her dress fell on both sides of her chair, puffing out full of folds, and reached the ground. When Leon occasionally felt the sole of his boot resting on it, he drew back as if he had trodden upon some one.

When the game of cards was over, the druggist and the Doctor played dominoes, and Emma, changing her place, leant her elbow on the table, turning over the leaves of "L'Illustration". She had brought her ladies' journal with her. Leon sat down near her; they looked at the engravings together, and waited for one another at the bottom of the pages. She often begged him to read her the verses; Leon declaimed them in a languid voice, to which he carefully gave a dying fall in the love passages. But the noise of the dominoes annoyed him. Monsieur Homais was strong at the game; he could beat Charles and give him a double-six. Then the three hundred finished, they both stretched themselves out in front of the fire, and were soon asleep. The fire was dying out in the cinders; the teapot was empty, Leon was still reading.

Emma listened to him, mechanically turning around the lampshade, on the gauze of which were painted clowns in carriages, and tight-rope dances with their balancing-poles. Leon stopped, pointing with a gesture to his sleeping audience; then they talked in low tones, and their conversation seemed the more sweet to them because it was unheard.

Thus a kind of bond was established between them, a constant commerce of books and of romances. Monsieur Bovary, little given to jealousy, did not trouble himself about it.

On his birthday he received a beautiful phrenological head, all marked with figures to the thorax and painted blue. This was an attention of the clerk's. He showed him many others, even to doing errands for him at Rouen; and the book of a novelist having made the mania for cactuses fashionable, Leon bought some for Madame Bovary, bringing them back on his knees in the "Hirondelle," pricking his fingers on their hard hairs.

She had a board with a balustrade fixed against her window to hold the pots. The clerk, too, had his small hanging garden; they saw each other tending their flowers at their windows.

Of the windows of the village there was one yet more often occupied; for on Sundays from morning to night, and every morning when the weather was bright, one could see at the dormer-window of the garret the profile of Monsieur Binet bending over his lathe, whose monotonous humming could be heard at the Lion d'Or.

One evening on coming home Leon found in his room a rug in velvet and wool with leaves on a pale ground. He called Madame Homais, Monsieur Homais, Justin, the children, the cook; he spoke of it to his chief; every one wanted to see this rug. Why did the doctor's wife give the clerk presents? It looked queer. They decided that she must be his lover.

He made this seem likely, so ceaselessly did he talk of her charms and of her wit; so much so, that Binet once roughly answered him—

"What does it matter to me since I'm not in her set?"

He tortured himself to find out how he could make his declaration to her, and always halting between the fear of displeasing her and the shame of being such a coward, he wept with discouragement and desire. Then he took energetic resolutions, wrote letters that he tore up, put it off to times that he again deferred.

Often he set out with the determination to dare all; but this resolution soon deserted him in Emma's presence, and when Charles, dropping in, invited him to jump into his chaise to go with him to see some patient in the neighbourhood, he at once accepted, bowed to madame, and went out. Her husband, was he not something belonging to her? As to

Emma, she did not ask herself whether she loved. Love, she thought, must come suddenly, with great outbursts and lightnings—a hurricane of the skies, which falls upon life, revolutionises it, roots up the will like a leaf, and sweeps the whole heart into the abyss. She did not know that on the terrace of houses it makes lakes when the pipes are choked, and she would thus have remained in her security when she suddenly discovered a rent in the wall of it.

Chapter 5

It was a Sunday in February, an afternoon when the snow was falling. They had all, Monsieur and Madame Bovary, Homais, and Monsieur Leon, gone to see a yarn-mill that was being built in the valley a mile and a half from Yonville. The druggist had taken Napoleon and Athalie to give them some exercise, and Justin accompanied them, carrying the umbrellas on his shoulder.

Nothing, however, could be less curious than this curiosity. A great piece of waste ground, on which pell-mell, amid a mass of sand and stones, were a few break-wheels, already rusty, surrounded by a quadrangular building pierced by a number of little windows. The building was unfinished; the sky could be seen through the joists of the roofing. Attached to the stop-plank of the gable a bunch of straw mixed with corn-ears fluttered its tricoloured ribbons in the wind.

Homais was talking. He explained to the company the future importance of this establishment, computed the strength of the floorings, the thickness of the walls, and regretted extremely not having a yard-stick such as Monsieur Binet possessed for his own special use.

Emma, who had taken his arm, bent lightly against his shoulder, and she looked at the sun's disc shedding afar through the mist his pale splendour. She turned. Charles was there. His cap was drawn down over his eyebrows, and his two thick lips were trembling, which added a look of stupidity to his face; his very back, his calm back, was irritating to behold, and she saw written upon his coat all the platitude of the bearer.

While she was considering him thus, tasting in her irritation a sort of depraved pleasure, Leon made a step forward. The cold that made him pale seemed to add a more gentle languor to his face; between his cravat and his neck the somewhat loose collar of his shirt showed the skin; the lobe of his ear looked out from beneath a lock of hair, and his large blue eyes, raised to the clouds, seemed to Emma more limpid and more beautiful than those mountain-lakes where the heavens are mirrored.

"Wretched boy!" suddenly cried the chemist.

And he ran to his son, who had just precipitated himself into a heap of lime in order to whiten his boots. At the reproaches with which he was being overwhelmed Napoleon began to roar, while Justin dried his shoes with a wisp of straw. But a knife was wanted; Charles offered his.

"Ah!" she said to herself, "he carried a knife in his pocket like a peasant."

The hoar-frost was falling, and they turned back to Yonville.

In the evening Madame Bovary did not go to her neighbour's, and when Charles had left and she felt herself alone, the comparison re-began with the clearness of a sensation almost actual, and with that lengthening of perspective which memory gives to things. Looking from her bed at the clean fire that was burning, she still saw, as she had down there, Leon standing up with one hand behind his cane, and with the other holding Athalie, who was quietly sucking a piece of ice. She thought him charming; she could not tear herself away from him; she recalled his other attitudes on other days, the words he had spoken, the sound of his voice, his whole person; and she repeated, pouting out her lips as if for a kiss—

"Yes, charming! charming! Is he not in love?" she asked herself; "but with whom? With me?"

All the proofs arose before her at once; her heart leapt. The flame of the fire threw a joyous light upon the ceiling; she turned on her back, stretching out her arms.

Then began the eternal lamentation: "Oh, if Heaven had not willed it! And why not? What prevented it?"

When Charles came home at midnight, she seemed to have just awakened, and as he made a noise undressing, she complained of a headache, then asked carelessly what had happened that evening.

"Monsieur Leon," he said, "went to his room early."

She could not help smiling, and she fell asleep, her soul filled with a new delight.

The next day, at dusk, she received a visit from Monsieur Lherueux, the draper. He was a man of ability, was this shopkeeper. Born a Gascon but bred a Norman, he grafted upon his southern volubility the cunning of the Cauchois. His fat, flabby, beardless face seemed dyed by a decoction of liquorice, and his white hair made even more vivid the keen brilliance of his small black eyes. No one knew what he had been formerly; a pedlar said some, a banker at Routot according to others. What was certain was that he made complex calculations in his head that would have frightened Binet himself. Polite to obsequiousness, he always held himself with his back bent in the position of one who bows or who invites.

After leaving at the door his hat surrounded with crape, he put down a green bandbox on the table, and began by complaining to madame, with many civilities, that he should have remained till that day without gaining her confidence. A poor shop like his was not made to attract a "fashionable lady"; he emphasized the words; yet she had only to command, and he would undertake to provide her with anything she might wish, either in haberdashery or linen, millinery or fancy goods, for he went to town regularly four times a month. He was connected with the best houses. You could speak of him at the "Trois Freres," at the "Barbe d'Or," or at the "Grand Sauvage"; all these gentlemen knew him as well as the insides of their pockets. To-day, then he had come to show madame, in passing, various articles he happened to have, thanks to the most rare opportunity. And he pulled out half-a-dozen embroidered collars from the box.

Madame Bovary examined them. "I do not require anything," she said.

Then Monsieur Lheureux delicately exhibited three Algerian scarves, several packets of English needles, a pair of straw slippers, and finally, four eggcups in cocoanut wood, carved in open work by convicts. Then, with both hands on the table, his neck stretched out, his figure bent forward, open-mouthed, he watched Emma's look, who was walking up and down undecided amid these goods. From time to time, as if to remove some dust, he filliped with his nail the silk of the scarves spread out at full length, and they rustled with a little noise, making in the green twilight the gold spangles of their tissue scintillate like little stars.

"How much are they?"

"A mere nothing," he replied, "a mere nothing. But there's no hurry; whenever it's convenient. We are not Jews."

She reflected for a few moments, and ended by again declining Monsieur Lheureux's offer. He replied quite unconcernedly—

"Very well. We shall understand one another by and by. I have always got on with ladies—if I didn't with my own!"

Emma smiled.

"I wanted to tell you," he went on good-naturedly, after his joke, "that it isn't the money I should trouble about. Why, I could give you some, if need be."

She made a gesture of surprise.

"Ah!" said he quickly and in a low voice, "I shouldn't have to go far to find you some, rely on that."

And he began asking after Pere Tellier, the proprietor of the "Cafe Francais," whom Monsieur Bovary was then attending.

"What's the matter with Pere Tellier? He coughs so that he shakes his whole house, and I'm afraid he'll soon want a deal covering rather than a flannel vest. He was such a rake as a young man! Those sort of people, madame, have not the least regularity; he's burnt up with brandy. Still it's sad, all the same, to see an acquaintance go off."

And while he fastened up his box he discoursed about the doctor's patients.

"It's the weather, no doubt," he said, looking frowningly at the floor, "that causes these illnesses. I, too, don't feel the thing. One of these days I shall even have to consult the doctor for a pain I have in my back. Well, good-bye, Madame Bovary. At your service; your very humble servant." And he closed the door gently.

Emma had her dinner served in her bedroom on a tray by the fireside; she was a long time over it; everything was well with her.

"How good I was!" she said to herself, thinking of the scarves.

She heard some steps on the stairs. It was Leon. She got up and took from the chest of drawers the first pile of dusters to be hemmed. When he came in she seemed very busy.

The conversation languished; Madame Bovary gave it up every few minutes, whilst he himself seemed quite embarrassed. Seated on a low chair near the fire, he turned round in his fingers the ivory thimble-case. She stitched on, or from time to time turned down the hem of the cloth with her nail. She did not speak; he was silent, captivated by her silence, as he would have been by her speech.

"Poor fellow!" she thought.

"How have I displeased her?" he asked himself.

At last, however, Leon said that he should have, one of these days, to go to Rouen on some office business.

"Your music subscription is out; am I to renew it?"

"No," she replied.

"Why?"

"Because—"

And pursing her lips she slowly drew a long stitch of grey thread.

This work irritated Leon. It seemed to roughen the ends of her fingers. A gallant phrase came into his head, but he did not risk it.

"Then you are giving it up?" he went on.

"What?" she asked hurriedly. "Music? Ah! yes! Have I not my house to look after, my husband to attend to, a thousand things, in fact, many duties that must be considered first?"

She looked at the clock. Charles was late. Then, she affected anxiety. Two or three times she even repeated, "He is so good!"

The clerk was fond of Monsieur Bovary. But this tenderness on his behalf astonished him unpleasantly; nevertheless he took up on his praises, which he said everyone was singing, especially the chemist.

"Ah! he is a good fellow," continued Emma.

"Certainly," replied the clerk.

And he began talking of Madame Homais, whose very untidy appearance generally made them laugh.

"What does it matter?" interrupted Emma. "A good housewife does not trouble about her appearance."

Then she relapsed into silence.

It was the same on the following days; her talks, her manners, everything changed. She took interest in the housework, went to church regularly, and looked after her servant with more severity.

She took Berthe from nurse. When visitors called, Felicite brought her in, and Madame Bovary undressed her to show off her limbs. She declared she adored children; this was her consolation, her joy, her passion, and she accompanied her caresses with lyrical outburst which would have reminded anyone but the Yonville people of Sachette in "Notre Dame de Paris."

When Charles came home he found his slippers put to warm near the fire. His waistcoat now never wanted lining, nor his shirt buttons, and it was quite a pleasure to see in the cupboard the night-caps arranged in piles of the same height. She no longer grumbled as formerly at taking a turn in the garden; what he proposed was always done, although she did not understand the wishes to which she submitted without a murmur; and when Leon saw him by his fireside after dinner, his two hands on his stomach, his two feet on the fender, his two cheeks red with feeding, his eyes moist with happiness, the child crawling along the carpet, and this woman with the slender waist who came behind his arm-chair to kiss his forehead: "What madness!" he said to himself. "And how to reach her!"

And thus she seemed so virtuous and inaccessible to him that he lost all hope, even the faintest. But by this renunciation he placed her on an extraordinary pinnacle. To him she stood outside those fleshly attributes from which he had nothing to obtain, and in his heart she rose ever, and became farther removed from him after the magnificent manner of an apotheosis that is taking wing. It was one of those pure feelings that do not interfere with life, that are cultivated because they are rare, and whose loss would afflict more than their passion rejoices.

Emma grew thinner, her cheeks paler, her face longer. With her black hair, her large eyes, her aquiline nose, her birdlike walk, and always silent now, did she not seem to be passing through life scarcely touching it, and to bear on her brow the vague impress of some divine destiny? She was so sad and so calm, at once so gentle and so reserved, that near her one felt oneself seized by an icy charm, as we shudder in churches at the perfume of the flowers mingling with the cold of the marble. The others even did not escape from this seduction. The chemist said—

"She is a woman of great parts, who wouldn't be misplaced in a sub-prefecture."

The housewives admired her economy, the patients her politeness, the poor her charity.

But she was eaten up with desires, with rage, with hate. That dress with the narrow folds hid a distracted fear, of whose torment those chaste lips said nothing. She was in love with Leon, and sought solitude that she might with the more ease delight in his image. The sight of his form troubled the voluptuousness of this mediation. Emma thrilled at the sound of his step; then in his presence the emotion subsided, and afterwards there remained to her only an immense astonishment that ended in sorrow.

Leon did not know that when he left her in despair she rose after he had gone to see him in the street. She concerned herself about his comings and goings; she watched his face; she invented quite a history to find an excuse for going to his room. The chemist's wife seemed happy to her to sleep under the same roof, and her thoughts constantly centered upon this house, like the "Lion d'Or" pigeons, who came there to dip their red feet and white wings in its gutters. But the more Emma recognised her love, the more she crushed it down, that it might not be evident, that she might make it less. She would have liked Leon to guess it, and she imagined chances, catastrophes that should facilitate this.

What restrained her was, no doubt, idleness and fear, and a sense of shame also. She thought she had repulsed him too much, that the time was past, that all was lost. Then, pride, and joy of being able to say to herself, "I am virtuous," and to look at herself in the glass taking resigned poses, consoled her a little for the sacrifice she believed she was making.

Then the lusts of the flesh, the longing for money, and the melancholy of passion all blended themselves into one suffering, and instead of turning her thoughts from it, she clave to it the more, urging herself to pain, and seeking everywhere occasion for it. She was irritated by an ill-served dish or by a half-open door; bewailed the velvets she had not, the happiness she had missed, her too exalted dreams, her narrow home.

What exasperated her was that Charles did not seem to notice her anguish. His conviction that he was making her happy seemed to her an imbecile insult, and his sureness on this point ingratitude. For whose sake, then was she virtuous? Was it not for him, the obstacle to all felicity, the cause of all misery, and, as it were, the sharp clasp of that complex strap that bucked her in on all sides.

On him alone, then, she concentrated all the various hatreds that resulted from her boredom, and every effort to diminish only augmented it; for this useless trouble was added to the other reasons for despair, and contributed still more to the separation between them. Her own gentleness to herself made her rebel against him. Domestic mediocrity drove her to lewd fancies, marriage tenderness to adulterous desires. She would have liked Charles to beat her, that she might have a better right to hate him, to revenge herself upon him. She was surprised sometimes at the atrocious conjectures that came into her thoughts, and she had to go on smiling, to hear repeated to her at all hours that she was happy, to pretend to be happy, to let it be believed.

Yet she had loathing of this hypocrisy. She was seized with the temptation to flee somewhere with Leon to try a new life; but at once a vague chasm full of darkness opened within her soul.

"Besides, he no longer loves me," she thought. "What is to become of me? What help is to be hoped for, what consolation, what solace?"

She was left broken, breathless, inert, sobbing in a low voice, with flowing tears.

"Why don't you tell master?" the servant asked her when she came in during these crises.

"It is the nerves," said Emma. "Do not speak to him of it; it would worry him."

"Ah! yes," Felicite went on, "you are just like La Guerine, Pere Guerin's daughter, the fisherman at Pollet, that I used to know at Dieppe before I came to you. She was so sad, so sad, to see her standing upright on the threshold of her house, she seemed to you like a winding-sheet spread out before the door. Her illness, it appears, was a kind of fog that she had in her head, and the doctors could not do anything, nor the priest

GUSTAVE FLAUBERT

either. When she was taken too bad she went off quite alone to the sea-shore, so that the customs officer, going his rounds, often found her lying flat on her face, crying on the shingle. Then, after her marriage, it went off, they say."

"But with me," replied Emma, "it was after marriage that it began."

Chapter 6

One evening when the window was open, and she, sitting by it, had been watching Lestiboudois, the beadle, trimming the box, she suddenly heard the Angelus ringing.

It was the beginning of April, when the primroses are in bloom, and a warm wind blows over the flower-beds newly turned, and the gardens, like women, seem to be getting ready for the summer fetes. Through the bars of the arbour and away beyond the river seen in the fields, meandering through the grass in wandering curves. The evening vapours rose between the leafless poplars, touching their outlines with a violet tint, paler and more transparent than a subtle gauze caught athwart their branches. In the distance cattle moved about; neither their steps nor their lowing could be heard; and the bell, still ringing through the air, kept up its peaceful lamentation.

With this repeated tinkling the thoughts of the young woman lost themselves in old memories of her youth and school-days. She remembered the great candlesticks that rose above the vases full of flowers on the altar, and the tabernacle with its small columns. She would have liked to be once more lost in the long line of white veils, marked off here and there by the stuff black hoods of the good sisters bending over their prie-Dieu. At mass on Sundays, when she looked up, she saw the gentle face of the Virgin amid the blue smoke of the rising incense. Then she was moved; she felt herself weak and quite deserted, like the down of a bird whirled by the tempest, and it was unconsciously that she went towards the church, included to no matter what devotions, so that her soul was absorbed and all existence lost in it.

On the Place she met Lestivoudois on his way back, for, in order not to shorten his day's labour, he preferred interrupting his work, then beginning it again, so that he rang the Angelus to suit his own convenience. Besides, the ringing over a little earlier warned the lads of catechism hour.

Already a few who had arrived were playing marbles on the stones of the cemetery. Others, astride the wall, swung their legs, kicking with their clogs the large nettles growing between the little enclosure and the newest graves. This was the only green spot. All the rest was but stones, always covered with a fine powder, despite the vestry-broom.

The children in list shoes ran about there as if it were an enclosure made for them. The shouts of their voices could be heard through the humming of the bell. This grew less and less with the swinging of the great rope that, hanging from the top of the belfry, dragged its end on the ground. Swallows flitted to and fro uttering little cries, cut the air with the edge of their wings, and swiftly returned to their yellow nests under the tiles of the coping. At the end of the church a lamp was burning, the wick of a night-light in a glass hung up. Its light from a distance looked like a white stain trembling in the oil. A long ray of the sun fell across the nave and seemed to darken the lower sides and the corners.

"Where is the cure?" asked Madame Bovary of one of the lads, who was amusing himself by shaking a swivel in a hole too large for it.

"He is just coming," he answered.

And in fact the door of the presbytery grated; Abbe Bournisien appeared; the children, pell-mell, fled into the church.

"These young scamps!" murmured the priest, "always the same!"

Then, picking up a catechism all in rags that he had struck with is foot, "They respect nothing!" But as soon as he caught sight of Madame Bovary, "Excuse me," he said; "I did not recognise you."

He thrust the catechism into his pocket, and stopped short, balancing the heavy vestry key between his two fingers.

The light of the setting sun that fell full upon his face paled the lasting of his cassock, shiny at the elbows, unravelled at the hem. Grease and tobacco stains followed along his broad chest the lines of the buttons, and grew more numerous the farther they were from his neckcloth, in which the massive folds of his red chin rested; this was dotted with yellow spots, that disappeared beneath the coarse hair of his greyish beard. He had just dined and was breathing noisily.

"How are you?" he added.

"Not well," replied Emma; "I am ill."

"Well, and so am I," answered the priest. "These first warm days weaken one most remarkably, don't they? But, after all, we are born to suffer, as St. Paul says. But what does Monsieur Bovary think of it?"

"He!" she said with a gesture of contempt.

"What!" replied the good fellow, quite astonished, "doesn't he prescribe something for you?"

"Ah!" said Emma, "it is no earthly remedy I need."

But the cure from time to time looked into the church, where the kneeling boys were shouldering one another, and tumbling over like packs of cards.

"I should like to know—" she went on.

"You look out, Riboudet," cried the priest in an angry voice; "I'll warm your ears, you imp!" Then turning to Emma, "He's Boudet the carpenter's son; his parents are well off, and let him do just as he pleases. Yet he could learn quickly if he would, for he is very sharp. And so sometimes for a joke I call him Riboudet (like the road one takes to go to Maromme) and I even say 'Mon Riboudet.' Ha! Ha! 'Mont Riboudet.' The other day I repeated that just to Monsignor, and he laughed at it; he condescended to laugh at it. And how is Monsieur Bovary?"

She seemed not to hear him. And he went on—

"Always very busy, no doubt; for he and I are certainly the busiest people in the parish. But he is doctor of the body," he added with a thick laugh, "and I of the soul."

She fixed her pleading eyes upon the priest. "Yes," she said, "you solace all sorrows."

"Ah! don't talk to me of it, Madame Bovary. This morning I had to go to Bas-Diauville for a cow that was ill; they thought it was under a spell. All their cows, I don't know how it is—But pardon me! Longuemarre and Boudet! Bless me! Will you leave off?"

And with a bound he ran into the church.

The boys were just then clustering round the large desk, climbing over the precentor's footstool, opening the missal; and others on tiptoe were just about to venture into the confessional. But the priest suddenly distributed a shower of cuffs among them. Seizing them by the collars of their coats, he lifted them from the ground, and deposited them on their knees on the stones of the choir, firmly, as if he meant planting them there.

"Yes," said he, when he returned to Emma, unfolding his large cotton handkerchief, one corner of which he put between his teeth, "farmers are much to be pitied."

"Others, too," she replied.

"Assuredly. Town-labourers, for example."

"It is not they—"

"Pardon! I've there known poor mothers of families, virtuous women, I assure you, real saints, who wanted even bread."

"But those," replied Emma, and the corners of her mouth twitched as she spoke, "those, Monsieur le Cure, who have bread and have no—"

"Fire in the winter," said the priest.

"Oh, what does that matter?"

"What! What does it matter? It seems to me that when one has firing and food—for, after all—"

"My God! my God!" she sighed.

"It is indigestion, no doubt? You must get home, Madame Bovary; drink a little tea, that will strengthen you, or else a glass of fresh water with a little moist sugar."

"Why?" And she looked like one awaking from a dream.

"Well, you see, you were putting your hand to your forehead. I thought you felt faint." Then, bethinking himself, "But you were asking me something? What was it? I really don't remember."

"I? Nothing! nothing!" repeated Emma.

And the glance she cast round her slowly fell upon the old man in the cassock. They looked at one another face to face without speaking.

"Then, Madame Bovary," he said at last, "excuse me, but duty first, you know; I must look after my good-for-nothings. The first communion will soon be upon us, and I fear we shall be behind after all. So after Ascension Day I keep them recta* an extra hour every Wednesday. Poor children! One cannot lead them too soon into the path of the Lord, as, moreover, he has himself recommended us to do by the mouth of his Divine Son. Good health to you, madame; my respects to your husband."

And he went into the church making a genuflexion as soon as he reached the door.

Emma saw him disappear between the double row of forms, walking with a heavy tread, his head a little bent over his shoulder, and with his two hands half-open behind him.

Then she turned on her heel all of one piece, like a statue on a pivot, and went homewards. But the loud voice of the priest, the clear voices of the boys still reached her ears, and went on behind her.

"Are you a Christian?"

"Yes, I am a Christian."

"What is a Christian?"

"He who, being baptized-baptized-baptized—"

She went up the steps of the staircase holding on to the banisters, and when she was in her room threw herself into an arm-chair.

The whitish light of the window-panes fell with soft undulations.

The furniture in its place seemed to have become more immobile, and to lose itself in the shadow as in an ocean of darkness. The fire

---

* On the straight and narrow path.

was out, the clock went on ticking, and Emma vaguely marvelled at this calm of all things while within herself was such tumult. But little Berthe was there, between the window and the work-table, tottering on her knitted shoes, and trying to come to her mother to catch hold of the ends of her apron-strings.

"Leave me alone," said the latter, putting her from her with her hand.

The little girl soon came up closer against her knees, and leaning on them with her arms, she looked up with her large blue eyes, while a small thread of pure saliva dribbled from her lips on to the silk apron.

"Leave me alone," repeated the young woman quite irritably.

Her face frightened the child, who began to scream.

"Will you leave me alone?" she said, pushing her with her elbow.

Berthe fell at the foot of the drawers against the brass handle, cutting her cheek, which began to bleed, against it. Madame Bovary sprang to lift her up, broke the bell-rope, called for the servant with all her might, and she was just going to curse herself when Charles appeared. It was the dinner-hour; he had come home.

"Look, dear!" said Emma, in a calm voice, "the little one fell down while she was playing, and has hurt herself."

Charles reassured her; the case was not a serious one, and he went for some sticking plaster.

Madame Bovary did not go downstairs to the dining-room; she wished to remain alone to look after the child. Then watching her sleep, the little anxiety she felt gradually wore off, and she seemed very stupid to herself, and very good to have been so worried just now at so little. Berthe, in fact, no longer sobbed.

Her breathing now imperceptibly raised the cotton covering. Big tears lay in the corner of the half-closed eyelids, through whose lashes one could see two pale sunken pupils; the plaster stuck on her cheek drew the skin obliquely.

"It is very strange," thought Emma, "how ugly this child is!"

When at eleven o'clock Charles came back from the chemist's shop, whither he had gone after dinner to return the remainder of the sticking-plaster, he found his wife standing by the cradle.

"I assure you it's nothing." he said, kissing her on the forehead. "Don't worry, my poor darling; you will make yourself ill."

He had stayed a long time at the chemist's. Although he had not seemed much moved, Homais, nevertheless, had exerted himself to buoy him up, to "keep up his spirits." Then they had talked of the various dangers that threaten childhood, of the carelessness of servants. Madame Homais knew something of it, having still upon her chest the marks left by a basin full of soup that a cook had formerly dropped on her pinafore, and her good parents took no end of trouble for her. The knives were not sharpened, nor the floors waxed; there were iron gratings to the windows and strong bars across the fireplace; the little Homais, in spite of their spirit, could not stir without someone watching them; at the slightest cold their father stuffed them with pectorals; and until they were turned four they all, without pity, had to wear wadded head-protectors. This, it is true, was a fancy of Madame Homais'; her husband was inwardly afflicted at it. Fearing the possible consequences of such compression to the intellectual organs. He even went so far as to say to her, "Do you want to make Caribs or Botocudos of them?"

Charles, however, had several times tried to interrupt the conversation. "I should like to speak to you," he had whispered in the clerk's ear, who went upstairs in front of him.

"Can he suspect anything?" Leon asked himself. His heart beat, and he racked his brain with surmises.

At last, Charles, having shut the door, asked him to see himself what would be the price at Rouen of a fine daguerreotypes. It was a sentimental surprise he intended for his wife, a delicate attention—his portrait in a frock-coat. But he wanted first to know "how much it would be." The inquiries would not put Monsieur Leon out, since he went to town almost every week.

Why? Monsieur Homais suspected some "young man's affair" at the bottom of it, an intrigue. But he was mistaken. Leon was after no love-making. He was sadder than ever, as Madame Lefrancois saw from the amount of food he left on his plate. To find out more about it she questioned the tax-collector. Binet answered roughly that he "wasn't paid by the police."

All the same, his companion seemed very strange to him, for Leon often threw himself back in his chair, and stretching out his arms, complained vaguely of life.

"It's because you don't take enough recreation," said the collector.

"What recreation?"

"If I were you I'd have a lathe."

"But I don't know how to turn," answered the clerk.

"Ah! that's true," said the other, rubbing his chin with an air of mingled contempt and satisfaction.

Leon was weary of loving without any result; moreover he was beginning to feel that depression caused by the repetition of the same kind of life, when no interest inspires and no hope sustains it. He was so bored with Yonville and its inhabitants, that the sight of certain persons, of certain houses, irritated him beyond endurance; and the chemist, good fellow though he was, was becoming absolutely unbearable to him. Yet the prospect of a new condition of life frightened as much as it seduced him.

This apprehension soon changed into impatience, and then Paris from afar sounded its fanfare of masked balls with the laugh of grisettes. As he was to finish reading there, why not set out at once? What prevented him? And he began making home-preparations; he arranged his occupations beforehand. He furnished in his head an apartment. He would lead an artist's life there! He would take lessons on the guitar! He would have a dressing-gown, a Basque cap, blue velvet slippers! He even already was admiring two crossed foils over his chimney-piece, with a death's head on the guitar above them.

The difficulty was the consent of his mother; nothing, however, seemed more reasonable. Even his employer advised him to go to some other chambers where he could advance more rapidly. Taking a middle course, then, Leon looked for some place as second clerk at Rouen; found none, and at last wrote his mother a long letter full of details, in which he set forth the reasons for going to live at Paris immediately. She consented.

He did not hurry. Every day for a month Hivert carried boxes, valises, parcels for him from Yonville to Rouen and from Rouen to Yonville; and when Leon had packed up his wardrobe, had his three arm-chairs restuffed, bought a stock of neckties, in a word, had made more preparations than for a voyage around the world, he put it off from week to week, until he received a second letter from his mother urging him to leave, since he wanted to pass his examination before the vacation.

When the moment for the farewells had come, Madame Homais wept, Justin sobbed; Homais, as a man of nerve, concealed his emotion; he wished to carry his friend's overcoat himself as far as the gate of the notary, who was taking Leon to Rouen in his carriage.

The latter had just time to bid farewell to Monsieur Bovary.

When he reached the head of the stairs, he stopped, he was so out of breath. As he came in, Madame Bovary arose hurriedly.

"It is I again!" said Leon.

"I was sure of it!"

She bit her lips, and a rush of blood flowing under her skin made her red from the roots of her hair to the top of her collar. She remained standing, leaning with her shoulder against the wainscot.

"The doctor is not here?" he went on.

"He is out." She repeated, "He is out."

Then there was silence. They looked at one another and their thoughts, confounded in the same agony, clung close together like two throbbing breasts.

"I should like to kiss Berthe," said Leon.

Emma went down a few steps and called Felicite.

He threw one long look around him that took in the walls, the decorations, the fireplace, as if to penetrate everything, carry away everything. But she returned, and the servant brought Berthe, who was swinging a windmill roof downwards at the end of a string. Leon kissed her several times on the neck.

"Good-bye, poor child! good-bye, dear little one! good-bye!" And he gave her back to her mother.

"Take her away," she said.

They remained alone—Madame Bovary, her back turned, her face pressed against a window-pane; Leon held his cap in his hand, knocking it softly against his thigh.

"It is going to rain," said Emma.

"I have a cloak," he answered.

"Ah!"

She turned around, her chin lowered, her forehead bent forward.

The light fell on it as on a piece of marble, to the curve of the eyebrows, without one's being able to guess what Emma was seeing on the horizon or what she was thinking within herself.

"Well, good-bye," he sighed.

She raised her head with a quick movement.

"Yes, good-bye—go!"

They advanced towards each other; he held out his hand; she hesitated.

"In the English fashion, then," she said, giving her own hand wholly to him, and forcing a laugh.

Leon felt it between his fingers, and the very essence of all his being seemed to pass down into that moist palm. Then he opened his hand; their eyes met again, and he disappeared.

When he reached the market-place, he stopped and hid behind a pillar to look for the last time at this white house with the four green blinds. He thought he saw a shadow behind the window in the room; but the curtain, sliding along the pole as though no one were touching it, slowly opened its long oblique folds that spread out with a single movement, and thus hung straight and motionless as a plaster wall. Leon set off running.

From afar he saw his employer's gig in the road, and by it a man in a coarse apron holding the horse. Homais and Monsieur Guillaumin were talking. They were waiting for him.

"Embrace me," said the druggist with tears in his eyes. "Here is your coat, my good friend. Mind the cold; take care of yourself; look after yourself."

"Come, Leon, jump in," said the notary.

Homais bent over the splash-board, and in a voice broken by sobs uttered these three sad words—

"A pleasant journey!"

"Good-night," said Monsieur Guillaumin. "Give him his head." They set out, and Homais went back.

Madame Bovary had opened her window overlooking the garden and watched the clouds. They gathered around the sunset on the side of Rouen and then swiftly rolled back their black columns, behind which the great rays of the sun looked out like the golden arrows of a suspended trophy, while the rest of the empty heavens was white as porcelain. But a gust of wind bowed the poplars, and suddenly the rain fell; it pattered against the green leaves.

Then the sun reappeared, the hens clucked, sparrows shook their wings in the damp thickets, and the pools of water on the gravel as they flowed away carried off the pink flowers of an acacia.

"Ah! how far off he must be already!" she thought.

Monsieur Homais, as usual, came at half-past six during dinner.

"Well," said he, "so we've sent off our young friend!"

"So it seems," replied the doctor. Then turning on his chair; "Any news at home?"

"Nothing much. Only my wife was a little moved this afternoon. You know women—a nothing upsets them, especially my wife. And we should be wrong to object to that, since their nervous organization is much more malleable than ours."

"Poor Leon!" said Charles. "How will he live at Paris? Will he get used to it?"

Madame Bovary sighed.

"Get along!" said the chemist, smacking his lips. "The outings at restaurants, the masked balls, the champagne—all that'll be jolly enough, I assure you."

"I don't think he'll go wrong," objected Bovary.

"Nor do I," said Monsieur Homais quickly; "although he'll have to do like the rest for fear of passing for a Jesuit. And you don't know what a life those dogs lead in the Latin quarter with actresses. Besides, students are thought a great deal of in Paris. Provided they have a few accomplishments, they are received in the best society; there are even ladies of the Faubourg Saint-Germain who fall in love with them, which subsequently furnishes them opportunities for making very good matches."

"But," said the doctor, "I fear for him that down there—"

"You are right," interrupted the chemist; "that is the reverse of the medal. And one is constantly obliged to keep one's hand in one's pocket there. Thus, we will suppose you are in a public garden. An individual presents himself, well dressed, even wearing an order, and whom one would take for a diplomatist. He approaches you, he insinuates himself; offers you a pinch of snuff, or picks up your hat. Then you become more intimate; he takes you to a cafe, invites you to his country-house, introduces you, between two drinks, to all sorts of people; and three-fourths of the time it's only to plunder your watch or lead you into some pernicious step.

"That is true," said Charles; "but I was thinking especially of illnesses—of typhoid fever, for example, that attacks students from the provinces."

Emma shuddered.

"Because of the change of regimen," continued the chemist, "and of the perturbation that results therefrom in the whole system. And then the water at Paris, don't you know! The dishes at restaurants, all the spiced food, end by heating the blood, and are not worth, whatever people may say of them, a good soup. For my own part, I have always preferred plain living; it is more healthy. So when I was studying pharmacy at Rouen, I boarded in a boarding house; I dined with the professors."

And thus he went on, expounding his opinions generally and his personal likings, until Justin came to fetch him for a mulled egg that was wanted.

"Not a moment's peace!" he cried; "always at it! I can't go out for a minute! Like a plough-horse, I have always to be moiling and toiling.

What drudgery!" Then, when he was at the door, "By the way, do you know the news?"

"What news?"

"That it is very likely," Homais went on, raising his eyebrows and assuming one of his most serious expression, "that the agricultural meeting of the Seine-Inferieure will be held this year at Yonville-l'Abbaye. The rumour, at all events, is going the round. This morning the paper alluded to it. It would be of the utmost importance for our district. But we'll talk it over later on. I can see, thank you; Justin has the lantern."

Chapter 7

The next day was a dreary one for Emma. Everything seemed to her enveloped in a black atmosphere floating confusedly over the exterior of things, and sorrow was engulfed within her soul with soft shrieks such as the winter wind makes in ruined castles. It was that reverie which we give to things that will not return, the lassitude that seizes you after everything was done; that pain, in fine, that the interruption of every wonted movement, the sudden cessation of any prolonged vibration, brings on.

As on the return from Vaubyessard, when the quadrilles were running in her head, she was full of a gloomy melancholy, of a numb despair. Leon reappeared, taller, handsomer, more charming, more vague. Though separated from her, he had not left her; he was there, and the walls of the house seemed to hold his shadow.

She could not detach her eyes from the carpet where he had walked, from those empty chairs where he had sat. The river still flowed on, and slowly drove its ripples along the slippery banks.

They had often walked there to the murmur of the waves over the moss-covered pebbles. How bright the sun had been! What happy afternoons they had seen alone in the shade at the end of the garden! He read aloud, bareheaded, sitting on a footstool of dry sticks; the fresh wind of the meadow set trembling the leaves of the book and the nasturtiums of the arbour. Ah! he was gone, the only charm of her life, the only possible hope of joy. Why had she not seized this happiness when it came to her? Why not have kept hold of it with both hands, with both knees, when it was about to flee from her? And she cursed herself for not having loved Leon. She thirsted for his lips. The wish took possession of her to run after and rejoin him, throw herself into his arms and say to him, "It is I; I am yours." But Emma recoiled beforehand at the difficulties of the enterprise, and her desires, increased by regret, became only the more acute.

Henceforth the memory of Leon was the centre of her boredom; it burnt there more brightly than the fire travellers have left on the snow of a Russian steppe. She sprang towards him, she pressed against him, she stirred carefully the dying embers, sought all around her anything that could revive it; and the most distant reminiscences, like the most immediate occasions, what she experienced as well as what she imagined, her voluptuous desires that were unsatisfied, her projects of happiness that crackled in the wind like dead boughs, her sterile virtue, her lost hopes, the domestic tete-a-tete—she gathered it all up, took everything, and made it all serve as fuel for her melancholy.

The flames, however, subsided, either because the supply had exhausted itself, or because it had been piled up too much. Love, little by little, was quelled by absence; regret stifled beneath habit; and this incendiary light that had empurpled her pale sky was overspread and faded by degrees. In the supineness of her conscience she even took her repugnance towards her husband for aspirations towards her lover, the burning of hate for the warmth of tenderness; but as the tempest still raged, and as passion burnt itself down to the very cinders, and no help came, no sun rose, there was night on all sides, and she was lost in the terrible cold that pierced her.

Then the evil days of Tostes began again. She thought herself now far more unhappy; for she had the experience of grief, with the certainty that it would not end.

A woman who had laid on herself such sacrifices could well allow herself certain whims. She bought a Gothic prie-dieu, and in a month spent fourteen francs on lemons for polishing her nails; she wrote to Rouen for a blue cashmere gown; she chose one of Lheureux's finest scarves, and wore it knotted around her waist over her dressing-gown; and, with closed blinds and a book in her hand, she lay stretched out on a couch in this garb.

She often changed her coiffure; she did her hair a la Chinoise, in flowing curls, in plaited coils; she parted in on one side and rolled it under like a man's.

She wanted to learn Italian; she bought dictionaries, a grammar, and a supply of white paper. She tried serious reading, history, and philosophy. Sometimes in the night Charles woke up with a start, thinking he was being called to a patient. "I'm coming," he stammered; and it was the noise of a match Emma had struck to relight the lamp. But her reading fared like her piece of embroidery, all of which, only just begun, filled her cupboard; she took it up, left it, passed on to other books.

She had attacks in which she could easily have been driven to commit any folly. She maintained one day, in opposition to her husband, that she could drink off a large glass of brandy, and, as Charles was stupid enough to dare her to, she swallowed the brandy to the last drop.

In spite of her vapourish airs (as the housewives of Yonville called them), Emma, all the same, never seemed gay, and usually she had at the corners of her mouth that immobile contraction that puckers the faces of old maids, and those of men whose ambition has failed. She was pale all over, white as a sheet; the skin of her nose was drawn at the nostrils, her eyes looked at you vaguely. After discovering three grey hairs on her temples, she talked much of her old age.

She often fainted. One day she even spat blood, and, as Charles fussed around her showing his anxiety—

"Bah!" she answered, "what does it matter?"

Charles fled to his study and wept there, both his elbows on the table, sitting in an arm-chair at his bureau under the phrenological head.

Then he wrote to his mother begging her to come, and they had many long consultations together on the subject of Emma.

What should they decide? What was to be done since she rejected all medical treatment? "Do you know what your wife wants?" replied Madame Bovary senior.

"She wants to be forced to occupy herself with some manual work. If she were obliged, like so many others, to earn her living, she wouldn't have these vapours, that come to her from a lot of ideas she stuffs into her head, and from the idleness in which she lives."

"Yet she is always busy," said Charles.

"Ah! always busy at what? Reading novels, bad books, works against religion, and in which they mock at priests in speeches taken from Voltaire. But all that leads you far astray, my poor child. Anyone who has no religion always ends by turning out badly."

So it was decided to stop Emma reading novels. The enterprise did not seem easy. The good lady undertook it. She was, when she passed through Rouen, to go herself to the lending-library and represent that Emma had discontinued her subscription. Would they not have a right to apply to the police if the librarian persisted all the same in his poisonous trade? The farewells of mother and daughter-in-law were cold. During the three weeks that they had been together they had not exchanged half-a-dozen words apart from the inquiries and phrases when they met at table and in the evening before going to bed.

Madame Bovary left on a Wednesday, the market-day at Yonville.

The Place since morning had been blocked by a row of carts, which, on end and their shafts in the air, spread all along the line of houses from the church to the inn. On the other side there were canvas booths, where cotton checks, blankets, and woollen stockings were sold, together with harness for horses, and packets of blue ribbon, whose ends fluttered in the wind. The coarse hardware was spread out on the ground between pyramids of eggs and hampers of cheeses, from which sticky straw stuck out.

Near the corn-machines clucking hens passed their necks through the bars of flat cages. The people, crowding in the same place and unwilling to move thence, sometimes threatened to smash the shop front of the chemist. On Wednesdays his shop was never empty, and the people pushed in less to buy drugs than for consultations. So great was Homais' reputation in the neighbouring villages. His robust aplomb had fascinated the rustics. They considered him a greater doctor than all the doctors.

Emma was leaning out at the window; she was often there. The window in the provinces replaces the theatre and the promenade, she was amusing herself with watching the crowd of boors when she saw a gentleman in a green velvet coat. He had on yellow gloves, although he wore heavy gaiters; he was coming towards the doctor's house, followed by a peasant walking with a bent head and quite a thoughtful air.

"Can I see the doctor?" he asked Justin, who was talking on the doorsteps with Felicite, and, taking him for a servant of the house—"Tell him that Monsieur Rodolphe Boulanger of La Huchette is here."

It was not from territorial vanity that the new arrival added "of La Huchette" to his name, but to make himself the better known.

La Huchette, in fact, was an estate near Yonville, where he had just bought the chateau and two farms that he cultivated himself, without, however, troubling very much about them. He lived as a bachelor, and was supposed to have "at least fifteen thousand francs a year."

Charles came into the room. Monsieur Boulanger introduced his man, who wanted to be bled because he felt "a tingling all over."

"That'll purge me," he urged as an objection to all reasoning.

So Bovary ordered a bandage and a basin, and asked Justin to hold it. Then addressing the peasant, who was already pale—

"Don't be afraid, my lad."

"No, no, sir," said the other; "get on."

And with an air of bravado he held out his great arm. At the prick of the lancet the blood spurted out, splashing against the looking-glass.

"Hold the basin nearer," exclaimed Charles.

"Lor!" said the peasant, "one would swear it was a little fountain flowing. How red my blood is! That's a good sign, isn't it?"

"Sometimes," answered the doctor, "one feels nothing at first, and then syncope sets in, and more especially with people of strong constitution like this man."

At these words the rustic let go the lancet-case he was twisting between his fingers. A shudder of his shoulders made the chair-back creak. His hat fell off.

"I thought as much," said Bovary, pressing his finger on the vein.

The basin was beginning to tremble in Justin's hands; his knees shook, he turned pale.

"Emma! Emma!" called Charles.

With one bound she came down the staircase.

"Some vinegar," he cried. "O dear! two at once!"

And in his emotion he could hardly put on the compress.

"It is nothing," said Monsieur Boulanger quietly, taking Justin in his arms. He seated him on the table with his back resting against the wall.

Madame Bovary began taking off his cravat. The strings of his shirt had got into a knot, and she was for some minutes moving her light fingers about the young fellow's neck. Then she poured some vinegar on her cambric handkerchief; she moistened his temples with little dabs, and then blew upon them softly. The ploughman revived, but Justin's syncope still lasted, and his eyeballs disappeared in the pale sclerotics like blue flowers in milk.

"We must hide this from him," said Charles.

Madame Bovary took the basin to put it under the table. With the movement she made in bending down, her dress (it was a summer dress with four flounces, yellow, long in the waist and wide in the skirt) spread out around her on the flags of the room; and as Emma stooping, staggered a little as she stretched out her arms.

The stuff here and there gave with the inflections of her bust.

Then she went to fetch a bottle of water, and she was melting some pieces of sugar when the chemist arrived. The servant had been to fetch him in the tumult. Seeing his pupil's eyes staring he drew a long breath; then going around him he looked at him from head to foot.

"Fool!" he said, "really a little fool! A fool in four letters! A phlebotomy's a big affair, isn't it! And a fellow who isn't afraid of anything; a kind of squirrel, just as he is who climbs to vertiginous heights to shake down nuts. Oh, yes! you just talk to me, boast about yourself! Here's a fine fitness for practising pharmacy later on; for under serious circumstances you may be called before the tribunals in order to enlighten the minds of the magistrates, and you would have to keep your head then, to reason, show yourself a man, or else pass for an imbecile."

Justin did not answer. The chemist went on—

"Who asked you to come? You are always pestering the doctor and madame. On Wednesday, moreover, your presence is indispensable to me. There are now twenty people in the shop. I left everything because of the interest I take in you. Come, get along! Sharp! Wait for me, and keep an eye on the jars."

When Justin, who was rearranging his dress, had gone, they talked for a little while about fainting-fits. Madame Bovary had never fainted.

"That is extraordinary for a lady," said Monsieur Boulanger; "but some people are very susceptible. Thus in a duel, I have seen a second lose consciousness at the mere sound of the loading of pistols."

"For my part," said the chemist, "the sight of other people's blood doesn't affect me at all, but the mere thought of my own flowing would make me faint if I reflected upon it too much."

Monsieur Boulanger, however, dismissed his servant, advising him to calm himself, since his fancy was over.

"It procured me the advantage of making your acquaintance," he added, and he looked at Emma as he said this. Then he put three francs on the corner of the table, bowed negligently, and went out.

He was soon on the other side of the river (this was his way back to La Huchette), and Emma saw him in the meadow, walking under the poplars, slackening his pace now and then as one who reflects.

"She is very pretty," he said to himself; "she is very pretty, this doctor's wife. Fine teeth, black eyes, a dainty foot, a figure like a Parisienne's. Where the devil does she come from? Wherever did that fat fellow pick her up?"

Monsieur Rodolphe Boulanger was thirty-four; he was of brutal temperament and intelligent perspicacity, having, moreover, had much to do with women, and knowing them well. This one had seemed pretty to him; so he was thinking about her and her husband.

"I think he is very stupid. She is tired of him, no doubt. He has dirty nails, and hasn't shaved for three days. While he is trotting after his patients, she sits there botching socks. And she gets bored! She would like to live in town and dance polkas every evening. Poor little woman! She is gaping after love like a carp after water on a kitchen-table. With three words of gallantry she'd adore one, I'm sure of it. She'd be tender, charming. Yes; but how to get rid of her afterwards?"

GUSTAVE FLAUBERT

Then the difficulties of love-making seen in the distance made him by contrast think of his mistress. She was an actress at Rouen, whom he kept; and when he had pondered over this image, with which, even in remembrance, he was satiated—

"Ah! Madame Bovary," he thought, "is much prettier, especially fresher. Virginie is decidedly beginning to grow fat. She is so finiky about her pleasures; and, besides, she has a mania for prawns."

The fields were empty, and around him Rodolphe only heard the regular beating of the grass striking against his boots, with a cry of the grasshopper hidden at a distance among the oats. He again saw Emma in her room, dressed as he had seen her, and he undressed her.

"Oh, I will have her," he cried, striking a blow with his stick at a clod in front of him. And he at once began to consider the political part of the enterprise. He asked himself—

"Where shall we meet? By what means? We shall always be having the brat on our hands, and the servant, the neighbours, and husband, all sorts of worries. Pshaw! one would lose too much time over it."

Then he resumed, "She really has eyes that pierce one's heart like a gimlet. And that pale complexion! I adore pale women!"

When he reached the top of the Arguiel hills he had made up his mind. "It's only finding the opportunities. Well, I will call in now and then. I'll send them venison, poultry; I'll have myself bled, if need be. We shall become friends; I'll invite them to my place. By Jove!" added he, "there's the agricultural show coming on. She'll be there. I shall see her. We'll begin boldly, for that's the surest way."

Chapter 8

At last it came, the famous agricultural show. On the morning of the solemnity all the inhabitants at their doors were chatting over the preparations. The pediment of the town hall had been hung with garlands of ivy; a tent had been erected in a meadow for the banquet; and in the middle of the Place, in front of the church, a kind of bombarde was to announce the arrival of the prefect and the names of the successful farmers who had obtained prizes. The National Guard of Buchy (there was none at Yonville) had come to join the corps of firemen, of whom Binet was captain. On that day he wore a collar even higher than usual; and, tightly buttoned in his tunic, his figure was so stiff and motionless that the whole vital portion of his person seemed to have descended into his legs, which rose in a cadence of set steps with a single movement. As there was some rivalry between the tax-collector and the colonel, both, to show off their talents, drilled their men separately. One saw the red epaulettes and the black breastplates pass and re-pass alternately; there was no end to it, and it constantly began again. There had never been such a display of pomp. Several citizens had scoured their houses the evening before; tri-coloured flags hung from half-open windows; all the public-houses were full; and in the lovely weather the starched caps, the golden crosses, and the coloured neckerchiefs seemed whiter than snow, shone in the sun, and relieved with the motley colours the sombre monotony of the frock-coats and blue smocks. The neighbouring farmers' wives, when they got off their horses, pulled out the long pins that fastened around them their dresses, turned up for fear of mud; and the husbands, for their part, in order to save their hats, kept their handkerchiefs around them, holding one corner between their teeth.

The crowd came into the main street from both ends of the village. People poured in from the lanes, the alleys, the houses; and from time to time one heard knockers banging against doors closing behind women with their gloves, who were going out to see the fete. What was most admired were two long lamp-stands covered with lanterns, that flanked a platform on which the authorities were to sit. Besides this there were against the four columns of the town hall four kinds of poles, each bearing a small standard of greenish cloth, embellished with inscriptions in gold letters.

On one was written, "To Commerce"; on the other, "To Agriculture"; on the third, "To Industry"; and on the fourth, "To the Fine Arts."

But the jubilation that brightened all faces seemed to darken that of Madame Lefrancois, the innkeeper. Standing on her kitchen-steps she muttered to herself, "What rubbish! what rubbish! With their canvas booth! Do they think the prefect will be glad to dine down there under a tent like a gipsy? They call all this fussing doing good to the place! Then it wasn't worth while sending to Neufchatel for the keeper of a cookshop! And for whom? For cowherds! tatterdemalions!"

The druggist was passing. He had on a frock-coat, nankeen trousers, beaver shoes, and, for a wonder, a hat with a low crown.

"Your servant! Excuse me, I am in a hurry." And as the fat widow asked where he was going—

"It seems odd to you, doesn't it, I who am always more cooped up in my laboratory than the man's rat in his cheese."

"What cheese?" asked the landlady.

"Oh, nothing! nothing!" Homais continued. "I merely wished to convey to you, Madame Lefrancois, that I usually live at home like a recluse. To-day, however, considering the circumstances, it is necessary—"

"Oh, you're going down there!" she said contemptuously.

"Yes, I am going," replied the druggist, astonished. "Am I not a member of the consulting commission?"

Mere Lefrancois looked at him for a few moments, and ended by saying with a smile—

"That's another pair of shoes! But what does agriculture matter to you? Do you understand anything about it?"

"Certainly I understand it, since I am a druggist—that is to say, a chemist. And the object of chemistry, Madame Lefrancois, being the knowledge of the reciprocal and molecular action of all natural bodies, it follows that agriculture is comprised within its domain. And, in fact, the composition of the manure, the fermentation of liquids, the analyses of gases, and the influence of miasmata, what, I ask you, is all this, if it isn't chemistry, pure and simple?"

The landlady did not answer. Homais went on—

"Do you think that to be an agriculturist it is necessary to have tilled the earth or fattened fowls oneself? It is necessary rather to know the composition of the substances in question—the geological strata, the atmospheric actions, the quality of the soil, the minerals, the waters, the density of the different bodies, their capillarity, and what not. And one must be master of all the principles of hygiene in order to direct, criticize the construction of buildings, the feeding of animals, the diet of domestics. And, moreover, Madame Lefrancois, one must know botany, be able to distinguish between plants, you understand, which are the wholesome and those that are deleterious, which are unproductive and which nutritive, if it is well to pull them up here and re-sow them there, to propagate some, destroy others; in brief, one must keep pace with science by means of pamphlets and public papers, be always on the alert to find out improvements."

The landlady never took her eyes off the "Cafe Francois" and the chemist went on—

"Would to God our agriculturists were chemists, or that at least they would pay more attention to the counsels of science. Thus lately I myself wrote a considerable tract, a memoir of over seventy-two pages, entitled, 'Cider, its Manufacture and its Effects, together with some New Reflections on the Subject,' that I sent to the Agricultural Society of Rouen, and which even procured me the honour of being received among its members—Section, Agriculture; Class, Pomological. Well, if my work had been given to the public—" But the druggist stopped, Madame Lefrancois seemed so preoccupied.

"Just look at them!" she said. "It's past comprehension! Such a cookshop as that!" And with a shrug of the shoulders that stretched out over her breast the stitches of her knitted bodice, she pointed with both hands at her rival's inn, whence songs were heard issuing. "Well, it won't last long," she added. "It'll be over before a week."

Homais drew back with stupefaction. She came down three steps and whispered in his ear—

"What! you didn't know it? There is to be an execution in next week. It's Lheureux who is selling him out; he has killed him with bills."

"What a terrible catastrophe!" cried the druggist, who always found expressions in harmony with all imaginable circumstances.

Then the landlady began telling him the story that she had heard from Theodore, Monsieur Guillaumin's servant, and although she detested Tellier, she blamed Lheureux. He was "a wheedler, a sneak."

"There!" she said. "Look at him! he is in the market; he is bowing to Madame Bovary, who's got on a green bonnet. Why, she's taking Monsieur Boulanger's arm."

"Madame Bovary!" exclaimed Homais. "I must go at once and pay her my respects. Perhaps she'll be very glad to have a seat in the enclosure under the peristyle." And, without heeding Madame Lefrancois, who was calling him back to tell him more about it, the druggist walked off rapidly with a smile on his lips, with straight knees, bowing copiously to right and left, and taking up much room with the large tails of his frock-coat that fluttered behind him in the wind.

Rodolphe, having caught sight of him from afar, hurried on, but Madame Bovary lost her breath; so he walked more slowly, and, smiling at her, said in a rough tone—

"It's only to get away from that fat fellow, you know, the druggist." She pressed his elbow.

"What's the meaning of that?" he asked himself. And he looked at her out of the corner of his eyes.

Her profile was so calm that one could guess nothing from it. It stood out in the light from the oval of her bonnet, with pale ribbons on it like the leaves of weeds. Her eyes with their long curved lashes looked straight before her, and though wide open, they seemed slightly puckered by the cheek-bones, because of the blood pulsing gently under the delicate skin. A pink line ran along the partition between her nostrils. Her head was bent upon her shoulder, and the pearl tips of her white teeth were seen between her lips.

"Is she making fun of me?" thought Rodolphe.

Emma's gesture, however, had only been meant for a warning; for Monsieur Lheureux was accompanying them, and spoke now and again as if to enter into the conversation.

"What a superb day! Everybody is out! The wind is east!"

And neither Madame Bovary nor Rodolphe answered him, whilst at the slightest movement made by them he drew near, saying, "I beg your pardon!" and raised his hat.

When they reached the farrier's house, instead of following the road up to the fence, Rodolphe suddenly turned down a path, drawing with him Madame Bovary. He called out—

"Good evening, Monsieur Lheureux! See you again presently."

"How you got rid of him!" she said, laughing.

"Why," he went on, "allow oneself to be intruded upon by others? And as to-day I have the happiness of being with you—"

Emma blushed. He did not finish his sentence. Then he talked of the fine weather and of the pleasure of walking on the grass. A few daisies had sprung up again.

"Here are some pretty Easter daisies," he said, "and enough of them to furnish oracles to all the amorous maids in the place."

He added, "Shall I pick some? What do you think?"

"Are you in love?" she asked, coughing a little.

"H'm, h'm! who knows?" answered Rodolphe.

The meadow began to fill, and the housewives hustled you with their great umbrellas, their baskets, and their babies. One had often to get out of the way of a long file of country folk, servant-maids with blue stockings, flat shoes, silver rings, and who smelt of milk, when one passed close to them. They walked along holding one another by the hand, and thus they spread over the whole field from the row of open trees to the banquet tent.

But this was the examination time, and the farmers one after the other entered a kind of enclosure formed by a long cord supported on sticks.

The beasts were there, their noses towards the cord, and making a confused line with their unequal rumps. Drowsy pigs were burrowing in the earth with their snouts, calves were bleating, lambs baaing; the cows, on knees folded in, were stretching their bellies on the grass, slowly chewing the cud, and blinking their heavy eyelids at the gnats that buzzed round them. Plough-men with bare arms were holding by the halter prancing stallions that neighed with dilated nostrils looking towards the mares. These stood quietly, stretching out their heads and flowing manes, while their foals rested in their shadow, or now and then came and sucked them. And above the long undulation of these crowded animals one saw some white mane rising in the wind like a wave, or some sharp horns sticking out, and the heads of men running about. Apart, outside the enclosure, a hundred paces off, was a large black bull, muzzled, with an iron ring in its nostrils, and who moved no more than if he had been in bronze. A child in rags was holding him by a rope.

Between the two lines the committee-men were walking with heavy steps, examining each animal, then consulting one another in a low voice. One who seemed of more importance now and then took notes in a book as he walked along. This was the president of the jury, Monsieur Derozerays de la Panville. As soon as he recognised Rodolphe he came forward quickly, and smiling amiably, said—

"What! Monsieur Boulanger, you are deserting us?"

Rodolphe protested that he was just coming. But when the president had disappeared—

"Ma foi!*" said he, "I shall not go. Your company is better than his."

---

* Upon my word!

GUSTAVE FLAUBERT

And while poking fun at the show, Rodolphe, to move about more easily, showed the gendarme his blue card, and even stopped now and then in front of some fine beast, which Madame Bovary did not at all admire. He noticed this, and began jeering at the Yonville ladies and their dresses; then he apologised for the negligence of his own. He had that incongruity of common and elegant in which the habitually vulgar think they see the revelation of an eccentric existence, of the perturbations of sentiment, the tyrannies of art, and always a certain contempt for social conventions, that seduces or exasperates them. Thus his cambric shirt with plaited cuffs was blown out by the wind in the opening of his waistcoat of grey ticking, and his broad-striped trousers disclosed at the ankle nankeen boots with patent leather gaiters.

These were so polished that they reflected the grass. He trampled on horses's dung with them, one hand in the pocket of his jacket and his straw hat on one side.

"Besides," added he, "when one lives in the country—"

"It's waste of time," said Emma.

"That is true," replied Rodolphe. "To think that not one of these people is capable of understanding even the cut of a coat!"

Then they talked about provincial mediocrity, of the lives it crushed, the illusions lost there.

"And I too," said Rodolphe, "am drifting into depression."

"You!" she said in astonishment; "I thought you very light-hearted."

"Ah! yes. I seem so, because in the midst of the world I know how to wear the mask of a scoffer upon my face; and yet, how many a time at the sight of a cemetery by moonlight have I not asked myself whether it were not better to join those sleeping there!"

"Oh! and your friends?" she said. "You do not think of them."

"My friends! What friends? Have I any? Who cares for me?" And he accompanied the last words with a kind of whistling of the lips.

But they were obliged to separate from each other because of a great pile of chairs that a man was carrying behind them. He was so overladen with them that one could only see the tips of his wooden shoes and the ends of his two outstretched arms. It was Lestiboudois, the gravedigger, who was carrying the church chairs about amongst the people. Alive to all that concerned his interests, he had hit upon this means of turning the show to account; and his idea was succeeding, for he no longer knew which way to turn. In fact, the villagers, who were hot, quarreled for these seats, whose straw smelt of incense, and they leant against the thick backs, stained with the wax of candles, with a certain veneration.

Madame Bovary again took Rodolphe's arm; he went on as if speaking to himself—

"Yes, I have missed so many things. Always alone! Ah! if I had some aim in life, if I had met some love, if I had found someone! Oh, how I would have spent all the energy of which I am capable, surmounted everything, overcome everything!"

"Yet it seems to me," said Emma, "that you are not to be pitied."

"Ah! you think so?" said Rodolphe.

"For, after all," she went on, "you are free—" she hesitated, "rich—"

"Do not mock me," he replied.

And she protested that she was not mocking him, when the report of a cannon resounded. Immediately all began hustling one another pell-mell towards the village.

It was a false alarm. The prefect seemed not to be coming, and the members of the jury felt much embarrassed, not knowing if they ought to begin the meeting or still wait.

At last at the end of the Place a large hired landau appeared, drawn by two thin horses, which a coachman in a white hat was whipping lustily. Binet had only just time to shout, "Present arms!" and the colonel to imitate him. All ran towards the enclosure; everyone pushed forward. A few even forgot their collars; but the equipage of the prefect seemed to anticipate the crowd, and the two yoked jades, trapesing in their harness, came up at a little trot in front of the peristyle of the town hall at the very moment when the National Guard and firemen deployed, beating drums and marking time.

"Present!" shouted Binet.

"Halt!" shouted the colonel. "Left about, march."

And after presenting arms, during which the clang of the band, letting loose, rang out like a brass kettle rolling downstairs, all the guns were lowered. Then was seen stepping down from the carriage a gentleman in a short coat with silver braiding, with bald brow, and wearing a tuft of hair at the back of his head, of a sallow complexion and the most benign appearance. His eyes, very large and covered by heavy lids, were half-closed to look at the crowd, while at the same time he raised his sharp nose, and forced a smile upon his sunken mouth. He recognised the mayor by his scarf, and explained to him that the prefect was not able to come. He himself was a councillor at the prefecture;

then he added a few apologies. Monsieur Tuvache answered them with compliments; the other confessed himself nervous; and they remained thus, face to face, their foreheads almost touching, with the members of the jury all round, the municipal council, the notable personages, the National Guard and the crowd. The councillor pressing his little cocked hat to his breast repeated his bows, while Tuvache, bent like a bow, also smiled, stammered, tried to say something, protested his devotion to the monarchy and the honour that was being done to Yonville.

Hippolyte, the groom from the inn, took the head of the horses from the coachman, and, limping along with his club-foot, led them to the door of the "Lion d'Or", where a number of peasants collected to look at the carriage. The drum beat, the howitzer thundered, and the gentlemen one by one mounted the platform, where they sat down in red utrecht velvet arm-chairs that had been lent by Madame Tuvache.

All these people looked alike. Their fair flabby faces, somewhat tanned by the sun, were the colour of sweet cider, and their puffy whiskers emerged from stiff collars, kept up by white cravats with broad bows. All the waist-coats were of velvet, double-breasted; all the watches had, at the end of a long ribbon, an oval cornelian seal; everyone rested his two hands on his thighs, carefully stretching the stride of their trousers, whose unsponged glossy cloth shone more brilliantly than the leather of their heavy boots.

The ladies of the company stood at the back under the vestibule between the pillars while the common herd was opposite, standing up or sitting on chairs. As a matter of fact, Lestiboudois had brought thither all those that he had moved from the field, and he even kept running back every minute to fetch others from the church. He caused such confusion with this piece of business that one had great difficulty in getting to the small steps of the platform.

"I think," said Monsieur Lheureux to the chemist, who was passing to his place, "that they ought to have put up two Venetian masts with something rather severe and rich for ornaments; it would have been a very pretty effect."

"To be sure," replied Homais; "but what can you expect? The mayor took everything on his own shoulders. He hasn't much taste. Poor Tuvache! and he is even completely destitute of what is called the genius of art."

Rodolphe, meanwhile, with Madame Bovary, had gone up to the first floor of the town hall, to the "council-room," and, as it was empty, he declared that they could enjoy the sight there more comfortably. He fetched three stools from the round table under the bust of the monarch, and having carried them to one of the windows, they sat down by each other.

There was commotion on the platform, long whisperings, much parleying. At last the councillor got up. They knew now that his name was Lieuvain, and in the crowd the name was passed from one to the other. After he had collated a few pages, and bent over them to see better, he began—

"Gentlemen! May I be permitted first of all (before addressing you on the object of our meeting to-day, and this sentiment will, I am sure, be shared by you all), may I be permitted, I say, to pay a tribute to the higher administration, to the government to the monarch, gentle men, our sovereign, to that beloved king, to whom no branch of public or private prosperity is a matter of indifference, and who directs with a hand at once so firm and wise the chariot of the state amid the incessant perils of a stormy sea, knowing, moreover, how to make peace respected as well as war, industry, commerce, agriculture, and the fine arts?"

"I ought," said Rodolphe, "to get back a little further."

"Why?" said Emma.

But at this moment the voice of the councillor rose to an extraordinary pitch. He declaimed—

"This is no longer the time, gentlemen, when civil discord ensanguined our public places, when the landlord, the business-man, the working-man himself, falling asleep at night, lying down to peaceful sleep, trembled lest he should be awakened suddenly by the noise of incendiary tocsins, when the most subversive doctrines audaciously sapped foundations."

"Well, someone down there might see me," Rodolphe resumed, "then I should have to invent excuses for a fortnight; and with my bad reputation—"

"Oh, you are slandering yourself," said Emma.

"No! It is dreadful, I assure you."

"But, gentlemen," continued the councillor, "if, banishing from my memory the remembrance of these sad pictures, I carry my eyes back to the actual situation of our dear country, what do I see there? Everywhere commerce and the arts are flourishing; everywhere new means of communication, like so many new arteries in the body of the state, establish within it new relations. Our great industrial centres have recovered all their activity; religion, more consolidated, smiles in all hearts; our ports are full, confidence is born again, and France breathes once more!"

"Besides," added Rodolphe, "perhaps from the world's point of view they are right."

"How so?" she asked.

"What!" said he. "Do you not know that there are souls constantly tormented? They need by turns to dream and to act, the purest passions and the most turbulent joys, and thus they fling themselves into all sorts of fantasies, of follies."

Then she looked at him as one looks at a traveller who has voyaged over strange lands, and went on—

"We have not even this distraction, we poor women!"

"A sad distraction, for happiness isn't found in it."

"But is it ever found?" she asked.

"Yes; one day it comes," he answered.

"And this is what you have understood," said the councillor.

"You, farmers, agricultural labourers! you pacific pioneers of a work that belongs wholly to civilization! you, men of progress and morality, you have understood, I say, that political storms are even more redoubtable than atmospheric disturbances!"

"It comes one day," repeated Rodolphe, "one day suddenly, and when one is despairing of it. Then the horizon expands; it is as if a voice cried, 'It is here!' You feel the need of confiding the whole of your life, of giving everything, sacrificing everything to this being. There is no need for explanations; they understand one another. They have seen each other in dreams!"

(And he looked at her.) "In fine, here it is, this treasure so sought after, here before you. It glitters, it flashes; yet one still doubts, one does not believe it; one remains dazzled, as if one went out from darkness into light."

And as he ended Rodolphe suited the action to the word. He passed his hand over his face, like a man seized with giddiness. Then he let it fall on Emma's. She took hers away.

"And who would be surprised at it, gentlemen? He only who is so blind, so plunged (I do not fear to say it), so plunged in the prejudices of another age as still to misunderstand the spirit of agricultural populations. Where, indeed, is to be found more patriotism than in the country, greater devotion to the public welfare, more intelligence, in a word? And, gentlemen, I do not mean that superficial intelligence, vain ornament of idle minds, but rather that profound and balanced intelligence that applies itself above all else to useful objects, thus contributing to the good of all, to the common amelioration and to the support of the state, born of respect for law and the practice of duty—"

"Ah! again!" said Rodolphe. "Always 'duty.' I am sick of the word. They are a lot of old blockheads in flannel vests and of old women with foot-warmers and rosaries who constantly drone into our ears 'Duty, duty!' Ah! by Jove! one's duty is to feel what is great, cherish the beautiful, and not accept all the conventions of society with the ignominy that it imposes upon us."

"Yet—yet—" objected Madame Bovary.

"No, no! Why cry out against the passions? Are they not the one beautiful thing on the earth, the source of heroism, of enthusiasm, of poetry, music, the arts, of everything, in a word?"

"But one must," said Emma, "to some extent bow to the opinion of the world and accept its moral code."

"Ah! but there are two," he replied. "The small, the conventional, that of men, that which constantly changes, that brays out so loudly, that makes such a commotion here below, of the earth earthly, like the mass of imbeciles you see down there. But the other, the eternal, that is about us and above, like the landscape that surrounds us, and the blue heavens that give us light."

Monsieur Lieuvain had just wiped his mouth with a pocket-handkerchief. He continued—

"And what should I do here gentlemen, pointing out to you the uses of agriculture? Who supplies our wants? Who provides our means of subsistence? Is it not the agriculturist? The agriculturist, gentlemen, who, sowing with laborious hand the fertile furrows of the country, brings forth the corn, which, being ground, is made into a powder by means of ingenious machinery, comes out thence under the name of flour, and from there, transported to our cities, is soon delivered at the baker's, who makes it into food for poor and rich alike. Again, is it not the agriculturist who fattens, for our clothes, his abundant flocks in the pastures? For how should we clothe ourselves, how nourish ourselves, without the agriculturist? And, gentlemen, is it even necessary to go so far for examples? Who has not frequently reflected on all the momentous things that we get out of that modest animal, the ornament of poultry-yards, that provides us at once with a soft pillow for our bed, with succulent flesh for our tables, and eggs? But I should never end if I were to enumerate one after the other all the different products which the earth, well cultivated, like a generous mother, lavishes upon her children. Here it is the vine,

GUSTAVE FLAUBERT

elsewhere the apple tree for cider, there colza, farther on cheeses and flax. Gentlemen, let us not forget flax, which has made such great strides of late years, and to which I will more particularly call your attention."

He had no need to call it, for all the mouths of the multitude were wide open, as if to drink in his words. Tuvache by his side listened to him with staring eyes. Monsieur Derozerays from time to time softly closed his eyelids, and farther on the chemist, with his son Napoleon between his knees, put his hand behind his ear in order not to lose a syllable. The chins of the other members of the jury went slowly up and down in their waistcoats in sign of approval. The firemen at the foot of the platform rested on their bayonets; and Binet, motionless, stood with out-turned elbows, the point of his sabre in the air. Perhaps he could hear, but certainly he could see nothing, because of the visor of his helmet, that fell down on his nose. His lieutenant, the youngest son of Monsieur Tuvache, had a bigger one, for his was enormous, and shook on his head, and from it an end of his cotton scarf peeped out. He smiled beneath it with a perfectly infantine sweetness, and his pale little face, whence drops were running, wore an expression of enjoyment and sleepiness.

The square as far as the houses was crowded with people. One saw folk leaning on their elbows at all the windows, others standing at doors, and Justin, in front of the chemist's shop, seemed quite transfixed by the sight of what he was looking at. In spite of the silence Monsieur Lieuvain's voice was lost in the air. It reached you in fragments of phrases, and interrupted here and there by the creaking of chairs in the crowd; then you suddenly heard the long bellowing of an ox, or else the bleating of the lambs, who answered one another at street corners. In fact, the cowherds and shepherds had driven their beasts thus far, and these lowed from time to time, while with their tongues they tore down some scrap of foliage that hung above their mouths.

Rodolphe had drawn nearer to Emma, and said to her in a low voice, speaking rapidly—

"Does not this conspiracy of the world revolt you? Is there a single sentiment it does not condemn? The noblest instincts, the purest sympathies are persecuted, slandered; and if at length two poor souls do meet, all is so organised that they cannot blend together. Yet they will make the attempt; they will flutter their wings; they will call upon each other. Oh! no matter. Sooner or later, in six months, ten years, they will come together, will love; for fate has decreed it, and they are born one for the other."

His arms were folded across his knees, and thus lifting his face towards Emma, close by her, he looked fixedly at her. She noticed in his eyes small golden lines radiating from black pupils; she even smelt the perfume of the pomade that made his hair glossy.

Then a faintness came over her; she recalled the Viscount who had waltzed with her at Vaubyessard, and his beard exhaled like this air an odour of vanilla and citron, and mechanically she half-closed her eyes the better to breathe it in. But in making this movement, as she leant back in her chair, she saw in the distance, right on the line of the horizon, the old diligence, the "Hirondelle," that was slowly descending the hill of Leux, dragging after it a long trail of dust. It was in this yellow carriage that Leon had so often come back to her, and by this route down there that he had gone for ever. She fancied she saw him opposite at his windows; then all grew confused; clouds gathered; it seemed to her that she was again turning in the waltz under the light of the lustres on the arm of the Viscount, and that Leon was not far away, that he was coming; and yet all the time she was conscious of the scent of Rodolphe's head by her side. This sweetness of sensation pierced through her old desires, and these, like grains of sand under a gust of wind, eddied to and fro in the subtle breath of the perfume which suffused her soul. She opened wide her nostrils several times to drink in the freshness of the ivy round the capitals. She took off her gloves, she wiped her hands, then fanned her face with her handkerchief, while athwart the throbbing of her temples she heard the murmur of the crowd and the voice of the councillor intoning his phrases. He said— "Continue, persevere; listen neither to the suggestions of routine, nor to the over-hasty councils of a rash empiricism.

"Apply yourselves, above all, to the amelioration of the soil, to good manures, to the development of the equine, bovine, ovine, and porcine races. Let these shows be to you pacific arenas, where the victor in leaving it will hold forth a hand to the vanquished, and will fraternise with him in the hope of better success. And you, aged servants, humble domestics, whose hard labour no Government up to this day has taken into consideration, come hither to receive the reward of your silent virtues, and be assured that the state henceforward has its eye upon you; that it encourages you, protects you; that it will accede to your just demands, and alleviate as much as in it lies the burden of your painful sacrifices."

Monsieur Lieuvain then sat down; Monsieur Derozerays got up, beginning another speech. His was not perhaps so florid as that of the councillor, but it recommended itself by a more direct style, that is to say, by more special knowledge and more elevated considerations. Thus the praise of the Government took up less space in it; religion and agriculture more. He showed in it the relations of these two, and how they had always contributed to civilisation. Rodolphe with Madame Bovary was talking dreams, presentiments, magnetism. Going back to the cradle of society, the orator painted those fierce times when men lived on acorns in the heart of woods. Then they had left off the skins of beasts, had put on cloth, tilled the soil, planted the vine. Was this a good, and in this discovery was there not more of injury than of gain? Monsieur Derozerays set himself this problem. From magnetism little by little Rodolphe had come to affinities, and while the president was citing Cincinnatus and his plough, Diocletian, planting his cabbages, and the Emperors of China inaugurating the year by the sowing of seed, the young man was explaining to the young woman that these irresistible attractions find their cause in some previous state of existence.

"Thus we," he said, "why did we come to know one another? What chance willed it? It was because across the infinite, like two streams that flow but to unite; our special bents of mind had driven us towards each other."

And he seized her hand; she did not withdraw it.

"For good farming generally!" cried the president.

"Just now, for example, when I went to your house."

"To Monsieur Bizat of Quincampoix."

"Did I know I should accompany you?"

"Seventy francs."

"A hundred times I wished to go; and I followed you—I remained."

"Manures!"

"And I shall remain to-night, to-morrow, all other days, all my life!"

"To Monsieur Caron of Argueil, a gold medal!"

"For I have never in the society of any other person found so complete a charm."

"To Monsieur Bain of Givry-Saint-Martin."

"And I shall carry away with me the remembrance of you."

"For a merino ram!"

"But you will forget me; I shall pass away like a shadow."

"To Monsieur Belot of Notre-Dame."

"Oh, no! I shall be something in your thought, in your life, shall I not?"

"Porcine race; prizes—equal, to Messrs. Leherisse and Cullembourg, sixty francs!"

Rodolphe was pressing her hand, and he felt it all warm and quivering like a captive dove that wants to fly away; but, whether she was trying to take it away or whether she was answering his pressure; she made a movement with her fingers. He exclaimed—

"Oh, I thank you! You do not repulse me! You are good! You understand that I am yours! Let me look at you; let me contemplate you!"

A gust of wind that blew in at the window ruffled the cloth on the table, and in the square below all the great caps of the peasant women were uplifted by it like the wings of white butterflies fluttering.

"Use of oil-cakes," continued the president. He was hurrying on: "Flemish manure-flax-growing-drainage-long leases-domestic service."

Rodolphe was no longer speaking. They looked at one another. A supreme desire made their dry lips tremble, and wearily, without an effort, their fingers intertwined.

"Catherine Nicaise Elizabeth Leroux, of Sassetot-la-Guerriere, for fifty-four years of service at the same farm, a silver medal—value, twenty-five francs!"

"Where is Catherine Leroux?" repeated the councillor.

She did not present herself, and one could hear voices whispering—

"Go up!"

"Don't be afraid!"

"Oh, how stupid she is!"

"Well, is she there?" cried Tuvache.

"Yes; here she is."

"Then let her come up!"

Then there came forward on the platform a little old woman with timid bearing, who seemed to shrink within her poor clothes. On her feet she wore heavy wooden clogs, and from her hips hung a large blue apron. Her pale face framed in a borderless cap was more wrinkled than a withered russet apple. And from the sleeves of her red jacket looked out two large hands with knotty joints, the dust of barns, the potash of washing the grease of wools had so encrusted, roughened, hardened these that they seemed dirty, although they had been rinsed in clear water; and by dint of long service they remained half open, as if to bear humble witness for themselves of so much suffering endured. Something of monastic rigidity dignified her face. Nothing of sadness or of emotion weakened that pale look. In her constant living with animals she had caught their dumbness and their calm. It was the first time that she found herself in the midst of so large a company, and inwardly scared by the flags, the drums, the gentlemen in frock-coats, and the order of the councillor, she stood motionless, not knowing whether to advance or run away, nor why the crowd was pushing her and the jury were smiling at her.

Thus stood before these radiant bourgeois this half-century of servitude.

"Approach, venerable Catherine Nicaise Elizabeth Leroux!" said the councillor, who had taken the list of prize-winners from the president; and, looking at the piece of paper and the old woman by turns, he repeated in a fatherly tone—"Approach! approach!"

"Are you deaf?" said Tuvache, fidgeting in his armchair; and he began shouting in her ear, "Fifty-four years of service. A silver medal! Twenty-five francs! For you!"

Then, when she had her medal, she looked at it, and a smile of beatitude spread over her face; and as she walked away they could hear her muttering "I'll give it to our cure up home, to say some masses for me!"

"What fanaticism!" exclaimed the chemist, leaning across to the notary.

The meeting was over, the crowd dispersed, and now that the speeches had been read, each one fell back into his place again, and everything into the old grooves; the masters bullied the servants, and these struck the animals, indolent victors, going back to the stalls, a green-crown on their horns.

The National Guards, however, had gone up to the first floor of the town hall with buns spitted on their bayonets, and the drummer of the battalion carried a basket with bottles. Madame Bovary took Rodolphe's arm; he saw her home; they separated at her door; then he walked about alone in the meadow while he waited for the time of the banquet.

The feast was long, noisy, ill served; the guests were so crowded that they could hardly move their elbows; and the narrow planks used for forms almost broke down under their weight. They ate hugely. Each one stuffed himself on his own account. Sweat stood on every brow, and a whitish steam, like the vapour of a stream on an autumn morning, floated above the table between the hanging lamps. Rodolphe, leaning against the calico of the tent was thinking so earnestly of Emma that he heard nothing. Behind him on the grass the servants were piling up the dirty plates, his neighbours were talking; he did not answer them; they filled his glass, and there was silence in his thoughts in spite of the growing noise. He was dreaming of what she had said, of the line of her lips; her face, as in a magic mirror, shone on the plates of the shakos, the folds of her gown fell along the walls, and days of love unrolled to all infinity before him in the vistas of the future.

He saw her again in the evening during the fireworks, but she was with her husband, Madame Homais, and the druggist, who was worrying about the danger of stray rockets, and every moment he left the company to go and give some advice to Binet.

The pyrotechnic pieces sent to Monsieur Tuvache had, through an excess of caution, been shut up in his cellar, and so the damp powder would not light, and the principal set piece, that was to represent a dragon biting his tail, failed completely. Now and then a meagre Roman-candle went off; then the gaping crowd sent up a shout that mingled with the cry of the women, whose waists were being squeezed in the darkness. Emma silently nestled against Charles's shoulder; then, raising her chin, she watched the luminous rays of the rockets against the dark sky. Rodolphe gazed at her in the light of the burning lanterns.

They went out one by one. The stars shone out. A few crops of rain began to fall. She knotted her fichu round her bare head.

At this moment the councillor's carriage came out from the inn.

His coachman, who was drunk, suddenly dozed off, and one could see from the distance, above the hood, between the two lanterns, the mass of his body, that swayed from right to left with the giving of the traces.

"Truly," said the druggist, "one ought to proceed most rigorously against drunkenness! I should like to see written up weekly at the door of the town hall on a board ad hoc* the names of all those who during the week got intoxicated on alcohol. Besides, with regard to statistics, one would thus have, as it were, public records that one could refer to in case of need. But excuse me!"

And he once more ran off to the captain. The latter was going back to see his lathe again.

"Perhaps you would not do ill," Homais said to him, "to send one of your men, or to go yourself—"

---

* Specifically for that.

"Leave me alone!" answered the tax-collector. "It's all right!"

"Do not be uneasy," said the druggist, when he returned to his friends. "Monsieur Binet has assured me that all precautions have been taken. No sparks have fallen; the pumps are full. Let us go to rest."

"Ma foi! I want it," said Madame Homais, yawning at large. "But never mind; we've had a beautiful day for our fete."

Rodolphe repeated in a low voice, and with a tender look, "Oh, yes! very beautiful!"

And having bowed to one another, they separated.

Two days later, in the "Final de Rouen," there was a long article on the show. Homais had composed it with verve the very next morning.

"Why these festoons, these flowers, these garlands? Whither hurries this crowd like the waves of a furious sea under the torrents of a tropical sun pouring its heat upon our heads?"

Then he spoke of the condition of the peasants. Certainly the Government was doing much, but not enough. "Courage!" he cried to it; "a thousand reforms are indispensable; let us accomplish them!" Then touching on the entry of the councillor, he did not forget "the martial air of our militia;" nor "our most merry village maidens;" nor the "bald-headed old men like patriarchs who were there, and of whom some, the remnants of our phalanxes, still felt their hearts beat at the manly sound of the drums." He cited himself among the first of the members of the jury, and he even called attention in a note to the fact that Monsieur Homais, chemist, had sent a memoir on cider to the agricultural society.

When he came to the distribution of the prizes, he painted the joy of the prize-winners in dithyrambic strophes. "The father embraced the son, the brother the brother, the husband his consort. More than one showed his humble medal with pride; and no doubt when he got home to his good housewife, he hung it up weeping on the modest walls of his cot.

"About six o'clock a banquet prepared in the meadow of Monsieur Leigeard brought together the principal personages of the fete. The greatest cordiality reigned here. Divers toasts were proposed: Monsieur Lieuvain, the King; Monsieur Tuvache, the Prefect; Monsieur Derozerays, Agriculture; Monsieur Homais, Industry and the Fine Arts, those twin sisters; Monsieur Leplichey, Progress. In the evening some brilliant fireworks on a sudden illumined the air. One would have called it a veritable kaleidoscope, a real operatic scene; and for a moment our little locality might have thought itself transported into the midst of a dream of the 'Thousand and One Nights.' Let us state that no untoward event disturbed this family meeting." And he added "Only the absence of the clergy was remarked. No doubt the priests understand progress in another fashion. Just as you please, messieurs the followers of Loyola!"

Chapter 9

Six weeks passed. Rodolphe did not come again. At last one evening he appeared.

The day after the show he had said to himself—"We mustn't go back too soon; that would be a mistake."

And at the end of a week he had gone off hunting. After the hunting he had thought it was too late, and then he reasoned thus—

"If from the first day she loved me, she must from impatience to see me again love me more. Let's go on with it!"

And he knew that his calculation had been right when, on entering the room, he saw Emma turn pale.

She was alone. The day was drawing in. The small muslin curtain along the windows deepened the twilight, and the gilding of the barometer, on which the rays of the sun fell, shone in the looking-glass between the meshes of the coral.

Rodolphe remained standing, and Emma hardly answered his first conventional phrases.

"I," he said, "have been busy. I have been ill."

"Seriously?" she cried.

"Well," said Rodolphe, sitting down at her side on a footstool, "no; it was because I did not want to come back."

"Why?"

"Can you not guess?"

He looked at her again, but so hard that she lowered her head, blushing. He went on—

"Emma!"

"Sir," she said, drawing back a little.

"Ah! you see," replied he in a melancholy voice, "that I was right not to come back; for this name, this name that fills my whole soul, and that escaped me, you forbid me to use! Madame Bovary! why all the world calls you thus! Besides, it is not your name; it is the name of another!"

He repeated, "of another!" And he hid his face in his hands.

"Yes, I think of you constantly. The memory of you drives me to despair. Ah! forgive me! I will leave you! Farewell! I will go far away, so far that you will never hear of me again; and yet—to-day—I know not what force impelled me towards you. For one does not struggle against

Heaven; one cannot resist the smile of angels; one is carried away by that which is beautiful, charming, adorable."

It was the first time that Emma had heard such words spoken to herself, and her pride, like one who reposes bathed in warmth, expanded softly and fully at this glowing language.

"But if I did not come," he continued, "if I could not see you, at least I have gazed long on all that surrounds you. At night-every night-I arose; I came hither; I watched your house, its glimmering in the moon, the trees in the garden swaying before your window, and the little lamp, a gleam shining through the window-panes in the darkness. Ah! you never knew that there, so near you, so far from you, was a poor wretch!"

She turned towards him with a sob.

"Oh, you are good!" she said.

"No, I love you, that is all! You do not doubt that! Tell me—one word—only one word!"

And Rodolphe imperceptibly glided from the footstool to the ground; but a sound of wooden shoes was heard in the kitchen, and he noticed the door of the room was not closed.

"How kind it would be of you," he went on, rising, "if you would humour a whim of mine." It was to go over her house; he wanted to know it; and Madame Bovary seeing no objection to this, they both rose, when Charles came in.

"Good morning, doctor," Rodolphe said to him.

The doctor, flattered at this unexpected title, launched out into obsequious phrases. Of this the other took advantage to pull himself together a little.

"Madame was speaking to me," he then said, "about her health."

Charles interrupted him; he had indeed a thousand anxieties; his wife's palpitations of the heart were beginning again. Then Rodolphe asked if riding would not be good.

"Certainly! excellent! just the thing! There's an idea! You ought to follow it up."

And as she objected that she had no horse, Monsieur Rodolphe offered one. She refused his offer; he did not insist. Then to explain his visit he said that his ploughman, the man of the blood-letting, still suffered from giddiness.

"I'll call around," said Bovary.

"No, no! I'll send him to you; we'll come; that will be more convenient for you."

"Ah! very good! I thank you."

And as soon as they were alone, "Why don't you accept Monsieur Boulanger's kind offer?"

She assumed a sulky air, invented a thousand excuses, and finally declared that perhaps it would look odd.

"Well, what the deuce do I care for that?" said Charles, making a pirouette. "Health before everything! You are wrong."

"And how do you think I can ride when I haven't got a habit?"

"You must order one," he answered.

The riding-habit decided her.

When the habit was ready, Charles wrote to Monsieur Boulanger that his wife was at his command, and that they counted on his good-nature.

The next day at noon Rodolphe appeared at Charles's door with two saddle-horses. One had pink rosettes at his ears and a deerskin side-saddle.

Rodolphe had put on high soft boots, saying to himself that no doubt she had never seen anything like them. In fact, Emma was charmed with his appearance as he stood on the landing in his great velvet coat and white corduroy breeches. She was ready; she was waiting for him.

Justin escaped from the chemist's to see her start, and the chemist also came out. He was giving Monsieur Boulanger a little good advice.

"An accident happens so easily. Be careful! Your horses perhaps are mettlesome."

She heard a noise above her; it was Felicite drumming on the windowpanes to amuse little Berthe. The child blew her a kiss; her mother answered with a wave of her whip.

"A pleasant ride!" cried Monsieur Homais. "Prudence! above all, prudence!" And he flourished his newspaper as he saw them disappear.

As soon as he felt the ground, Emma's horse set off at a gallop.

Rodolphe galloped by her side. Now and then they exchanged a word. Her figure slightly bent, her hand well up, and her right arm stretched out, she gave herself up to the cadence of the movement that rocked her in her saddle. At the bottom of the hill Rodolphe gave his horse its head; they started together at a bound, then at the top suddenly the horses stopped, and her large blue veil fell about her.

It was early in October. There was fog over the land. Hazy clouds hovered on the horizon between the outlines of the hills; others, rent asunder, floated up and disappeared. Sometimes through a rift in the clouds, beneath a ray of sunshine, gleamed from afar the roots of Yonville, with the gardens at the water's edge, the yards, the walls and the church steeple. Emma half closed her eyes to pick out her house, and never had this poor village where she lived appeared so small. From the height on which they were the whole valley seemed an immense pale lake sending off its vapour into the air. Clumps of trees here and there stood out like black rocks, and the tall lines of the poplars that rose above the mist were like a beach stirred by the wind.

By the side, on the turf between the pines, a brown light shimmered in the warm atmosphere. The earth, ruddy like the powder of tobacco, deadened the noise of their steps, and with the edge of their shoes the horses as they walked kicked the fallen fir cones in front of them.

Rodolphe and Emma thus went along the skirt of the wood. She turned away from time to time to avoid his look, and then she saw only the pine trunks in lines, whose monotonous succession made her a little giddy. The horses were panting; the leather of the saddles creaked.

Just as they were entering the forest the sun shone out.

"God protects us!" said Rodolphe.

"Do you think so?" she said.

"Forward! forward!" he continued.

He "tchk'd" with his tongue. The two beasts set off at a trot.

Long ferns by the roadside caught in Emma's stirrup.

Rodolphe leant forward and removed them as they rode along. At other times, to turn aside the branches, he passed close to her, and Emma felt his knee brushing against her leg. The sky was now blue, the leaves no longer stirred. There were spaces full of heather in flower, and plots of violets alternated with the confused patches of the trees that were grey, fawn, or golden coloured, according to the nature of their leaves. Often in the thicket was heard the fluttering of wings, or else the hoarse, soft cry of the ravens flying off amidst the oaks.

They dismounted. Rodolphe fastened up the horses. She walked on in front on the moss between the paths. But her long habit got in her way, although she held it up by the skirt; and Rodolphe, walking behind her, saw between the black cloth and the black shoe the fineness of her white stocking, that seemed to him as if it were a part of her nakedness.

She stopped. "I am tired," she said.

"Come, try again," he went on. "Courage!"

Then some hundred paces farther on she again stopped, and through her veil, that fell sideways from her man's hat over her hips, her face appeared in a bluish transparency as if she were floating under azure waves.

"But where are we going?"

He did not answer. She was breathing irregularly. Rodolphe looked round him biting his moustache. They came to a larger space where the coppice had been cut. They sat down on the trunk of a fallen tree, and Rodolphe began speaking to her of his love. He did not begin by frightening her with compliments. He was calm, serious, melancholy.

Emma listened to him with bowed head, and stirred the bits of wood on the ground with the tip of her foot. But at the words, "Are not our destinies now one?"

"Oh, no!" she replied. "You know that well. It is impossible!" She rose to go. He seized her by the wrist. She stopped. Then, having gazed at him for a few moments with an amorous and humid look, she said hurriedly—

"Ah! do not speak of it again! Where are the horses? Let us go back."

He made a gesture of anger and annoyance. She repeated:

"Where are the horses? Where are the horses?"

Then smiling a strange smile, his pupil fixed, his teeth set, he advanced with outstretched arms. She recoiled trembling. She stammered:

"Oh, you frighten me! You hurt me! Let me go!"

"If it must be," he went on, his face changing; and he again became respectful, caressing, timid. She gave him her arm. They went back. He said—

"What was the matter with you? Why? I do not understand. You were mistaken, no doubt. In my soul you are as a Madonna on a pedestal, in a place lofty, secure, immaculate. But I need you to live! I must have your eyes, your voice, your thought! Be my friend, my sister, my angel!"

And he put out his arm round her waist. She feebly tried to disengage herself. He supported her thus as they walked along.

But they heard the two horses browsing on the leaves.

"Oh! one moment!" said Rodolphe. "Do not let us go! Stay!"

He drew her farther on to a small pool where duckweeds made a greenness on the water. Faded water lilies lay motionless between the reeds. At the noise of their steps in the grass, frogs jumped away to hide themselves.

"I am wrong! I am wrong!" she said. "I am mad to listen to you!"

"Why? Emma! Emma!"

"Oh, Rodolphe!" said the young woman slowly, leaning on his shoulder.

The cloth of her habit caught against the velvet of his coat. She threw back her white neck, swelling with a sigh, and faltering, in tears, with a long shudder and hiding her face, she gave herself up to him—

The shades of night were falling; the horizontal sun passing between the branches dazzled the eyes. Here and there around her, in the leaves or on the ground, trembled luminous patches, as it hummingbirds flying about had scattered their feathers. Silence was everywhere; something sweet seemed to come forth from the trees; she felt her heart, whose beating had begun again, and the blood coursing through her flesh like a stream of milk. Then far away, beyond the wood, on the other hills, she heard a vague prolonged cry, a voice which lingered, and in silence she heard it mingling like music with the last pulsations of her throbbing nerves. Rodolphe, a cigar between his lips, was mending with his penknife one of the two broken bridles.

They returned to Yonville by the same road. On the mud they saw again the traces of their horses side by side, the same thickets, the same stones to the grass; nothing around them seemed changed; and yet for her something had happened more stupendous than if the mountains had moved in their places. Rodolphe now and again bent forward and took her hand to kiss it.

She was charming on horseback—upright, with her slender waist, her knee bent on the mane of her horse, her face somewhat flushed by the fresh air in the red of the evening.

On entering Yonville she made her horse prance in the road. People looked at her from the windows.

At dinner her husband thought she looked well, but she pretended not to hear him when he inquired about her ride, and she remained sitting there with her elbow at the side of her plate between the two lighted candles.

"Emma!" he said.

"What?"

"Well, I spent the afternoon at Monsieur Alexandre's. He has an old cob, still very fine, only a little broken-kneed, and that could be bought; I am sure, for a hundred crowns." He added, "And thinking it might please you, I have bespoken it—bought it. Have I done right? Do tell me?"

She nodded her head in assent; then a quarter of an hour later—

"Are you going out to-night?" she asked.

"Yes. Why?"

"Oh, nothing, nothing, my dear!"

And as soon as she had got rid of Charles she went and shut herself up in her room.

At first she felt stunned; she saw the trees, the paths, the ditches, Rodolphe, and she again felt the pressure of his arm, while the leaves rustled and the reeds whistled.

But when she saw herself in the glass she wondered at her face. Never had her eyes been so large, so black, of so profound a depth. Something subtle about her being transfigured her. She repeated, "I have a lover! a lover!" delighting at the idea as if a second puberty had come to her. So at last she was to know those joys of love, that fever of happiness of which she had despaired! She was entering upon marvels where all would be passion, ecstasy, delirium. An azure infinity encompassed her, the heights of sentiment sparkled under her thought, and ordinary existence appeared only afar off, down below in the shade, through the interspaces of these heights.

Then she recalled the heroines of the books that she had read, and the lyric legion of these adulterous women began to sing in her memory with the voice of sisters that charmed her. She became herself, as it were, an actual part of these imaginings, and realised the love-dream of her youth as she saw herself in this type of amorous women whom she had so envied. Besides, Emma felt a satisfaction of revenge. Had she not suffered enough? But now she triumphed, and the love so long pent up burst forth in full joyous bubblings. She tasted it without remorse, without anxiety, without trouble.

The day following passed with a new sweetness. They made vows to one another She told him of her sorrows. Rodolphe interrupted her with kisses; and she looking at him through half-closed eyes, asked him to call her again by her name—to say that he loved her They were in the forest, as yesterday, in the shed of some woodenshoe maker. The walls were of straw, and the roof so low they had to stoop. They were seated side by side on a bed of dry leaves.

From that day forth they wrote to one another regularly every evening. Emma placed her letter at the end of the garden, by the river, in a fissure of the wall. Rodolphe came to fetch it, and put another there, that she always found fault with as too short.

One morning, when Charles had gone out before day break, she was seized with the fancy to see Rodolphe at once. She would go quickly to La Huchette, stay there an hour, and be back again at Yonville while everyone was still asleep. This idea made her pant with desire, and she soon found herself in the middle of the field, walking with rapid steps, without looking behind her.

Day was just breaking. Emma from afar recognised her lover's house. Its two dove-tailed weathercocks stood out black against the pale dawn.

Beyond the farmyard there was a detached building that she thought must be the chateau She entered—it was if the doors at her approach had opened wide of their own accord. A large straight staircase led up to the corridor. Emma raised the latch of a door, and suddenly at the end of the room she saw a man sleeping. It was Rodolphe. She uttered a cry.

"You here? You here?" he repeated. "How did you manage to come? Ah! your dress is damp."

"I love you," she answered, throwing her arms about his neck.

This first piece of daring successful, now every time Charles went out early Emma dressed quickly and slipped on tiptoe down the steps that led to the waterside.

But when the plank for the cows was taken up, she had to go by the walls alongside of the river; the bank was slippery; in order not to fall she caught hold of the tufts of faded wallflowers. Then she went across ploughed fields, in which she sank, stumbling; and clogging her thin shoes. Her scarf, knotted round her head, fluttered to the wind in the meadows. She was afraid of the oxen; she began to run; she arrived out of breath, with rosy cheeks, and breathing out from her whole person a fresh perfume of sap, of verdure, of the open air. At this hour Rodolphe still slept. It was like a spring morning coming into his room.

The yellow curtains along the windows let a heavy, whitish light enter softly. Emma felt about, opening and closing her eyes, while the drops of dew hanging from her hair formed, as it were, a topaz aureole around her face. Rodolphe, laughing, drew her to him, and pressed her to his breast.

Then she examined the apartment, opened the drawers of the tables, combed her hair with his comb, and looked at herself in his shaving-glass. Often she even put between her teeth the big pipe that lay on the table by the bed, amongst lemons and pieces of sugar near a bottle of water.

It took them a good quarter of an hour to say goodbye. Then Emma cried. She would have wished never to leave Rodolphe. Something stronger than herself forced her to him; so much so, that one day, seeing her come unexpectedly, he frowned as one put out.

"What is the matter with you?" she said. "Are you ill? Tell me!"

At last he declared with a serious air that her visits were becoming imprudent—that she was compromising herself.

Chapter 10

Gradually Rodolphe's fears took possession of her. At first, love had intoxicated her; and she had thought of nothing beyond. But now that he was indispensable to her life, she feared to lose anything of this, or even that it should be disturbed. When she came back from his house she looked all about her, anxiously watching every form that passed in the horizon, and every village window from which she could be seen. She listened for steps, cries, the noise of the ploughs, and she stopped short, white, and trembling more than the aspen leaves swaying overhead.

One morning as she was thus returning, she suddenly thought she saw the long barrel of a carbine that seemed to be aimed at her. It stuck out sideways from the end of a small tub half-buried in the grass on the edge of a ditch. Emma, half-fainting with terror, nevertheless walked on, and a man stepped out of the tub like a Jack-in-the-box. He had gaiters buckled up to the knees, his cap pulled down over his eyes, trembling lips, and a red nose. It was Captain Binet lying in ambush for wild ducks.

"You ought to have called out long ago!" he exclaimed; "When one sees a gun, one should always give warning."

The tax-collector was thus trying to hide the fright he had had, for a prefectorial order having prohibited duckhunting except in boats, Monsieur Binet, despite his respect for the laws, was infringing them, and so he every moment expected to see the rural guard turn up. But this anxiety whetted his pleasure, and, all alone in his tub, he congratulated himself on his luck and on his cuteness. At sight of Emma he seemed relieved from a great weight, and at once entered upon a conversation.

"It isn't warm; it's nipping."

Emma answered nothing. He went on—

"And you're out so early?"

"Yes," she said stammering; "I am just coming from the nurse where my child is."

"Ah! very good! very good! For myself, I am here, just as you see me, since break of day; but the weather is so muggy, that unless one had the bird at the mouth of the gun—"

"Good evening, Monsieur Binet," she interrupted him, turning on her heel.

"Your servant, madame," he replied drily; and he went back into his tub.